From the Library of
St. Gabriel
Birthday Book Club

KRISTIE LAMM
September 20, 1980

Charlotte Shakespeare and Annie the Great

Charlotte Shakespeare

and

Annie the Great

by Barbara Ware Holmes

illustrated by John Himmelman

HARPER & ROW, PUBLISHERS   NEW YORK
Grand Rapids, Philadelphia, St. Louis, San Francisco
London, Singapore, Sydney, Tokyo, Toronto

Typography by Joyce Hopkins
1   2   3   4   5   6   7   8   9   10
First Edition

Library of Congress Cataloging-in-Publication Data
Holmes, Barbara Ware.
    Charlotte Shakespeare and Annie the Great / by Barbara Ware Holmes;
illustrated by John Himmelman.
        p.   cm.
    Summary: After prodding her best friend Annie into trying out for
the lead in the play she has written for their sixth grade class,
Charlotte feels herself losing control of her own play and
experiences jealousy when Annie suddenly gets all the attention.
    ISBN 0-06-022614-5 : $. —ISBN 0-06-022615-3 (lib. bdg.) : $
    [1. Plays—Fiction.   2. Authorship—Fiction.   3. Schools—Fiction.
4. Friendship—Fiction.]   I. Himmelman, John, ill.   II. Title.
PZ7.H7337Chp 1989
[Fic]—dc19
                                                                89-2037
                                                                CIP
                                                                AC

for
David

The author wishes to thank three people:
John and Mary Vest, of Roanoke, Virginia,
for "loaning" her Sam;
and Joshua Wood, of Southampton Township
School in Vincentown, New Jersey,
for helping with the title.

Charlotte
Shakespeare
and
Annie the Great

1

"When the curtain opens, it will be very dark onstage. And quiet." Charlotte lowered her voice. Annie nodded, respectfully silent. "All you'll hear is the rattling of skeleton bones and the cackling of a mean old witch."

Annie raised her eyebrows.

"Then—" Charlotte paused. She sighed. Then what? Witches? Ghosts? Same old Halloween stuff you always saw. There wouldn't be another scary minute in the whole play. What would be scary about seeing Tina and Laura and Jenny marching around in dumb witch costumes?

"What?" Annie asked. "Then *what*?"

Charlotte dropped her head onto her arms. Beneath her nose were the clean, unused pages of her notebook. "I don't know," she said drearily.

"That's as far as I got." Her voice echoed inside her arms.

There was silence from across the room. Charlotte knew what Annie was thinking. She'd had all summer to write this play. It was important, too. No one at school had ever been asked to write the sixth-grade play before.

She lifted her head. "I *tried!*" she protested. "All summer I tried. But it's *hard*! I'm not going to write just any old thing, like I did with my book!" Her novel had been gross. She'd written the most disgusting stuff she could think of, to get attention. She wanted this play to be *real*. A work of art. And she wanted Annie to have the lead. Nothing good ever happened to Annie.

4

Charlotte was going to make her a star, even though Annie didn't know it yet.

"I'm busy, Pippi," Charlotte said irritably to her cat. Pippi had pounced onto the desk and was marching back and forth across the notebook. With a plop, she sat down on top of it and lifted her chin. She purred. Charlotte was supposed to scratch her ears. Honestly! That was all cats had to think about. Charlotte smiled.

"Good thing you're not black," she said. "I'd put you in the play." She scratched the left ear first. Pippi's favorite.

Annie giggled. "Maybe she can be dyed."

Charlotte felt a little thump of excitement. Hey! Maybe she could. Fur was like hair, and hair could be dyed. A live cat—now *that* would be different!

Pippi suddenly leaped to the floor, her hind legs brushing Charlotte's face as she went. She wasn't stage material, Charlotte admitted, picking cat hairs from her mouth. If she wanted a real cat, it would have to be so old and lazy it couldn't move. But that wouldn't be scary.

This play was going to stink.

All morning Annie helped her think. It was no use. All the good Halloween ideas had been used. Even Annie agreed.

"What'll you do?" Annie asked worriedly.

"Mrs. Sanchez expects something great. Everyone does."

Charlotte nodded miserably. The sixth-grade teacher had decided Charlotte was a creative genius. Charlotte had thought so too at the time. She'd even been *excited* about writing this play. It was her chance to create a "thing of beauty and a joy forever." That's what a work of art was. Her dad and Mrs. Arnold had explained it all to her. But her dad had graduated from art school, and Mrs. Arnold was a librarian who'd read a million books. To them, it might sound easy to write a work of art, but it wasn't. So far, it was the hardest thing she'd ever done, and she hadn't even done it yet.

"Let's go eat." Charlotte stood up. At least eating would be *doing* something, and doing was better than thinking. Especially when you had no thoughts.

Charlotte's father was in the kitchen making himself a sandwich. There were red splotches of paint on his face and hands. He always got this way in the summer, when he had lots of time to paint. Other fathers got tans, hers got dots.

He smiled at them. "Want one?" he asked, holding up a sandwich. "My treat."

Annie nodded and blushed. She adored Charlotte's dad. If he offered her arsenic soup, she'd gulp it down and say "Thanks." Her father *was* great, Charlotte admitted. Famous, too. Just last week there had been an article about his paintings in the paper and a picture of him in his painting clothes, without the dots. But that only made things worse. Her ideas would never be as good as his. According to the paper, he was a "rare original in a mediocre world."

"What a morning," the rare original said tiredly, handing them each a sandwich, then draping himself over a chair to eat his own. "I think there's nothing but dust passing through this old brain."

Charlotte watched him with interest. That was exactly how *she* felt.

"It must be hard to get ideas," Annie said shyly, shooting Charlotte a sidelong glance. "For a work of art."

Mr. Cheetham nodded and took a bite. "It is. Getting started is the worst part. Somehow, once you get going, ideas come. It's just getting that first one rolling, you know?"

Annie and Charlotte both nodded.

"I had a problem like that," Charlotte said carefully, looking intently at her sandwich and picking off crust. "When I started my play. I couldn't think of a good idea for weeks. It seemed like all witches were the same."

Her father chuckled. "The ones I know certainly aren't! So. What did you do? Wait! Don't tell me! You put them in a real-life situation and they sprang to life. Right?"

Charlotte didn't look at Annie. Or her dad. She'd peeled off so much crust there was a little mountain on her plate and hardly any bread around her meat. "Right!"

Her father chuckled again. "And let me guess. Now you have one naughty little witch who lies."

Charlotte stopped peeling and looked up. Was her father making fun of her? *She* used to tell lies. Lots of them. But even as she wondered, the question fell away, and the little witch who lied moved into its place. Charlotte could see her at once. She knew how she'd act and what she'd say. Even her chants and spells would be made up and wouldn't work!

Charlotte looked slyly at Annie. They smiled.

"How did you know?" she asked casually.

"Good artists draw on what they know," her father said, brushing crumbs from the table into his cupped hand and carrying them to the sink. "We creative geniuses are all alike."

"This will be so funny, Charlotte," Annie said when they were back at work in the bedroom. "A little witch like you. The *old* you," she added.

Charlotte searched frantically through her desk to find a pen. Her mind was popping with ideas she wanted to write down, fast. "Think of the trouble she'll cause," she said elatedly. "People will believe her chants and try to use them!"

Annie frowned. "Will she be a good witch or bad?"

"Good, of course. Only her lies cause so much trouble you'd never know it."

Annie nodded. "And in the end she'll have to learn not to lie." She and Charlotte blushed at the same time. "Nothing personal," she added.

2

Mrs. Cheetham poured spaghetti into a collander and then into a bowl. She carried it to the table. Marie followed, carrying sauce. It had been Marie's turn to make dinner, but she'd forgotten a few things—noodles to go under the sauce, for one. Charlotte didn't know why her mother put up with Marie. She even made excuses for her and said things like "seventh graders have a lot on their minds." Well, *Charlotte* had a lot on her mind, but she remembered noodles when she cooked. Even Ruth, when she was in the seventh grade, had remembered noodles, and Ruth was pretty dumb.

"It's Ruth's fault I forgot," Marie said. "She was playing her Bon Jovi tape. I hate Bon Jovi."

Ruth glared at her sister. She opened her mouth to speak.

"Come on girls," Mrs. Cheetham said swiftly. "It was just a mistake. Let's forget it and eat."

"Before we *starve*," Ruth added. She managed to look near death already.

Mr. Cheetham passed Ruth the spaghetti. "You know," he said, leaning across the table to look in her face, "I'd like to have a peaceful meal for a change. Do you think we might manage that?"

Ruth didn't reply. She heaped spaghetti onto her plate and began to eat. As Mr. Cheetham passed the bowl to Charlotte, Ruth narrowed her eyes meanly at the back of his head.

Charlotte ignored Ruth. *She* could help them have a peaceful meal. She had too many things to think about to take part in dinner conversation. Her little witch, Carlotta, had told three big lies already. The plot thickened. Charlotte smiled. Now Ruth glared at *her*, as if the smile were a personal insult. Honestly, Ruth was acting weirder and weirder these days. It seemed like the older she got, the younger she acted. At this rate she'd be wearing diapers by the tenth grade. Charlotte smiled even more. Ruth glared even more.

"And what is so funny?" Ruth demanded.

Charlotte didn't reply. She could practically *see* Ruth in diapers. That funny throwaway kind with the plastic tape. Pampers. She laughed out loud.

"I *said* what's so funny?" Ruth kicked the table leg. Everyone looked up.

Charlotte tried desperately to stop smiling. If this wasn't a peaceful meal now, it would seem like her fault, even though it wasn't. But she couldn't help it. She imagined Ruth on the side of a Pampers box, wearing only a diaper. The king-size kind. Charlotte covered her mouth with both hands.

Ruth's look of anger suddenly disappeared. She began to look smug. "Go ahead," she said. "Smile. You won't be smiling soon. Maybe as soon as this weekend you won't be smiling at all."

And what did that mean? Charlotte looked at

her sister suspiciously. Ruth smirked.

"Ruth," Mr. Cheetham said with a frown. "You'd better not be doing what I think you're doing."

"I didn't tell her," Ruth said righteously. "I didn't say a word about it."

Mr. Cheetham buried his forehead in his hands.

Charlotte looked from Ruth to her dad and back to Ruth, who looked much too pleased with herself. Something big was going on. "Okay. What didn't she tell me that will make me not smile?" she demanded.

"Oh, for crying out loud." Mrs. Cheetham laid down her fork. She looked angrily at Ruth. "That she's getting a bird," she said. "Though I'm hardly in the mood to buy her one now."

"Mom!" Ruth sat up very straight. "I *didn't* tell her. You did!"

Charlotte stared at her mother in disbelief. She stared at her father. Wait a minute here. Were they talking about a *live* bird? The kind that cats like to eat? Ruth couldn't have a bird. Not with Pippi living in the house!

"She can't have a bird," Charlotte pointed out. "I have a cat."

"That's right!" Ruth looked smugger than ever. "You have a pet, so I can too. Dad agreed."

Charlotte flushed. Ruth didn't even want a bird! This was another one of her jealousy fits. Ever since Charlotte had started writing, Ruth had decided their father liked Charlotte best. You couldn't even mention the words "creative genius" when Ruth was around. So now Ruth had to have everything Charlotte had and even more. Charlotte was surprised she hadn't asked for a rhinoceros.

Mr. Cheetham laid both of his hands flat on the table. They all knew what that meant. No one spoke. "Ruth," he said, looking his eldest daughter in the eye. "This is not a contest, and it never was. If I even suspected you thought so, you would not be getting a bird." Ruth blushed.

"And Charlotte." He turned his gaze on her. "Ruth will keep the bird in her bedroom in a cage. It won't bother you or Pippi at all."

Charlotte bit her lip to keep from replying. Of course it would bother them. A lot!

"It will bother *me*," Marie said. Charlotte looked at her gratefully. "I *loathe* birds." She carried her plate to the sink, turning her toes out as she walked. It was her ballerina walk. Charlotte knew it was only an act. Two years of ballet lessons didn't make your toes turn out. But from now on Charlotte wouldn't say a word about it. Marie could walk any way she liked.

"And *I* loathe phony ballerinas," Ruth shouted.

Mr. and Mrs. Cheetham looked at each other.

"I loathe dinnertime," Mrs. Cheetham said wearily. "How about you?"

Charlotte stared at Annie while she read. Charlotte had written four whole scenes already. Every time Annie smiled, Charlotte leaned over to see where she was.

"Have you gotten to the red dots?" Charlotte asked eagerly.

Annie nodded and chuckled. She turned the page.

"Do you like the dot-me-magic part?"

Annie smiled. She just read on.

Charlotte couldn't stand it. She remembered the time they'd all gone to see her father's paintings hanging in a show at the university. There'd been people standing around talking and pointing at the pictures with her father right there in the room. He must have felt like this—like he'd break into pieces if somebody even frowned.

Annie would *have* to like the dot-me-magic. It was the best part. Carlotta told all the other little witches they didn't have to learn magic anymore. Studying was *so* old-fashioned. Modern witches could just buy the witchcraft in a little round tube

15

and dot it right on. Charlotte hoped some mothers would donate their old lipsticks to the play. Her mother wouldn't, of course, because she didn't wear any.

Annie slapped the notebook shut. Her eyes glowed.

"Well?" Charlotte insisted. "Do you like it, or not?" She could tell from Annie's face that she did, but Charlotte wanted her to say it.

Annie hugged the notebook to her chest. "This is wonderful, Charlotte," she whispered slowly. She shook her head in awe. "It's the best play I ever read or heard or saw in my whole life."

A lump grew in Charlotte's throat. Her friend looked so small and serious sitting there hugging the play. "Did you like the chant?" she asked shyly. She wanted to hear details: every single thought Annie had had about every single part.

Annie smiled. She lifted her chin:

> "Dot me here, and dot me there,
> Dot me, dot me, everywhere,
> Through my skin and underwear,
> Dot-me-magic—if you dare!"

If Charlotte had had any doubts that her friend could be the star, they vanished now. Inside all her shyness, Annie was just like Carlotta—funny and smart and a little sneaky, too. In a good way, though. She figured out how to make things work.

"You'll be a great Carlotta, Annie!" Charlotte said.

Annie stared at Charlotte. She slowly grew pale. "I'm not going to be Carlotta," she said. "I can't even act!"

Charlotte smiled. "Oh, yes you can!"

Annie sank down on Charlotte's bed. She looked stricken. "Don't say that, Charlotte," she said. "I don't want to be in this play! I don't want to be in *any* play, ever!"

Charlotte folded her arms and stared at her friend. "Do you know who's been planning to be the lead in the sixth-grade play for the last six years?" she asked.

Annie hung her head. Of course she knew. Tina, the rat.

"Do you think I'm writing a great play so that Tina can have the lead?"

Annie didn't look up. She bit her lip and didn't reply.

"I wrote this play for you," Charlotte said. "Because you're the smartest, nicest, most talented kid in school. Only nobody knows it."

Annie managed to shake her head. "No I'm not, Charlotte," she said weakly.

Charlotte carried her notebook back to her desk

and went to work. Annie would be a wonderful witch. She just had to get used to the idea. And get over being shy. This might be Annie's only chance in life. If someone like Charlotte didn't push her into being a star, it would be too late. She'd grow up and go to work at an ordinary job and nobody would ever know how special she was. Annie Block was *great*.

Charlotte snuck a look at her. Annie the Great sat on Charlotte's bed looking numb. She just needed a little push into greatness. One little, very hard push.

3

Four more days until school. Charlotte stared into her notebook. Okay. Cute little Carlotta had told all her lies. The plot was thick. Now what? Her father had said getting started was the hard part. Keeping going was hard too. Charlotte picked up her notebook and rushed downstairs.

She peeked into her father's studio. He was in there, painting. They weren't supposed to disturb him unless it was an emergency. This was definitely an emergency.

"Help!" Charlotte hollered from the doorway. Her father looked up, startled, and then frowned. Uh-oh. Maybe it *wasn't* an emergency.

"There's nothing but dust in this old brain," she hurried to say, remembering his words last week when he couldn't paint. Words he would

19

understand. They worked. Her father smiled.

"Experiment," he said when she'd explained. He leaned close to his easel and painted out a perfectly good apple. "Just go write. See what happens."

"I did, but it wasn't any good. I write, throw it away, write, throw it away. It's hard!"

Her father laughed. "Tell me about it. You know, I have twenty-year-old students who think they're going to be the next Picasso just because they have a little flair. A little flair isn't all it takes. A little flair and a *lot* of work—then you have something."

Charlotte barely heard. It was fascinating, watching her father's canvas. A new apple appeared in place of the old one. This one was green. "What's flair?" she asked suspiciously. She usually loved these artist-to-artist talks, but this one sounded a lot like a lecture.

Her father paused. "Flair is—well, talent, I guess. A special knack you're born with that's all your own. Artists have to have it, no doubt about that. But flair is only the start. You have to work to develop it into something serious and real. See this apple?" Charlotte nodded. Her father painted it out again. "This apple has looked ten different ways in one morning. I have to find the *right* way. I can't find it if I don't work. Experiment. Try different ways. Now just go into your

20

room and write. Read what you write out loud. You'll know when it's right."

Charlotte sighed. She was only eleven. It seemed like flair should be enough for now.

Her father suddenly stepped back from the easel and smiled. His apple looked very good in a moldy sort of way. He glowed his approval. Charlotte knew just how he felt—she'd felt the same way when she'd come up with the dot-me-magic chant. "Go on," he said. "Charlotte Shakespeare can do it."

Charlotte Shakespeare went back to her room to try. Any good creative genius would, she supposed.

The play was getting better and better. Annie came every day to read the latest scene. Every day she turned pale.

"This isn't like me," she'd say when she finished reading. "I'm not Carlotta at all."

"You don't have to *be* like her," Charlotte always explained. "You just have to *act*."

"And I can't *act*," Annie always replied.

Charlotte ignored her. Annie was going to do it. Why else would she rush over here every day? Deep down inside she was getting ready.

On the first day of school, Charlotte waited on the corner where she and Annie always met. She hugged the notebook with the play tightly to her chest. She couldn't wait to show Mrs. Sanchez! Her father had read the play last night and called it art. He'd meant it, too. Her father wouldn't lie about something like that. Charlotte jiggled impatiently. Where was Annie?

Suddenly, Annie rounded the corner. She looked different. Sort of—electric. She stopped in front of Charlotte and scowled.

"What you said isn't true!" she exploded. "Jenny or Laura could do it. They'd be great Carlottas and you know it, Charlotte! It doesn't have to be me or Tina. You only wanted me to think that so I'd feel bad and do it. It was a trick!"

For a second Charlotte didn't know what to say. It *had* been a trick. But for Annie's own good! And it wasn't really a trick, because nobody would take the part from Tina. Tina would kill Laura or Jenny if they did. And Sarah wouldn't try. So it *was* Tina or Annie, just like she'd said.

"Laura and Jenny wouldn't dare, and you know it," she said. "They're Tina's friends."

Annie's glare wavered. She began to walk. "Well, how do you know you'll get to pick parts, anyway?" she asked sulkily. "Mrs. Sanchez might pick them. Or she might hold tryouts. Yes. I think that's what she does."

Well, sure, it was what she'd done before. But

22

before she hadn't had Charlotte writing the play. She'd just picked one from some book. How could she not let Charlotte pick parts for her own play?

"If she holds tryouts, I'm not going to try," Annie said stubbornly. "And besides, you shouldn't pick me because I'm your friend. Kids will think you cheat."

Charlotte stopped walking. Suddenly she was furious. She knew kids would think that and it wasn't what she was doing at all. You couldn't use art for a selfish reason. Her father had told her that. She was picking Annie because she was best. And Annie wasn't even grateful.

"I picked you because you're best!" Charlotte shouted. "And Mrs. Sanchez will agree. She has to. She made me director, and directors are boss. If she wants this play, she gets you with it. Annie Block or NO PLAY!"

They stared at each other in surprise. Neither of them had expected Charlotte to say *that*. "You're blackmailing the teacher?" Annie croaked.

Charlotte hadn't thought so, but yes, maybe she was. If she had to, she would. For the good of the play—and art.

A smile began to spread slowly across Annie's face. She giggled. Charlotte tried not to giggle back, but she did. She couldn't help it.

Mrs. Sanchez was so anxious to get at the play, she practically knocked Peter over.

"Oh, Charlotte," she said cheerfully, thumbing through it. "Have I looked forward to this! How did it go?"

"Pretty well," Charlotte said as modestly as she could. "It's got lots of funny parts."

"Oh, good! Audiences love humor." The teacher ran her hand approvingly across the red binder. "May I take it home?"

Of course she could! Charlotte nodded.

"It may be the weekend before I have a chance to read it," Mrs. Sanchez warned. "I want to give it my undivided attention."

Charlotte was disappointed. She wanted the teacher to read it *now*. But that was dumb, of course. She couldn't read it in school. And undivided attention was worth waiting for. Peter and Tina, who'd moved close to eavesdrop, both frowned. They hated Charlotte to have any attention, especially the undivided kind.

"Sure," Charlotte said pleasantly. "That would be fine."

4

On Saturday, Ruth bought the bird. The owner of the pet shop had made Ruth visit it until it got used to her. Charlotte had felt a burst of hope, hearing this. No bird could ever get used to Ruth. But here it was, moving in. It must have really wanted a home.

Everyone gathered in Ruth's room. Charlotte could see right away why Ruth had picked it: It was big. Not as big as a parrot, but bigger than those little parakeets and canaries most people had. And it needed a bigger cage, of course. Well, bigger wasn't always better! Parakeets came in much better colors.

"It's a cockatiel," Ruth said proudly.

Charlotte studied it. She had to admit the thing wasn't bad. There was an interesting clump of

25

feathers on top of its head and it had bright-orange cheeks with a touch of yellow on its face. Mostly, though, it was gray. Dull. Of course Pippi was gray, but on cats gray looked good.

"So what's it do?" Marie asked.

Ruth smiled. "It sings," she said in a superior tone of voice. Charlotte's fifth-grade teacher, Miss Brown, had talked that way. It made you not want to listen to a single word. "This is a hand-tamed cockatiel that will grow very attached to its owner. That's *me*. And I'll be teaching it to talk."

Mrs. Cheetham stuck a finger through the bars of the cage. "Aren't you pretty?" she said. The bird fluttered frantically to the swing on the far side. The feathers on its head fanned out.

"Mom!" Ruth protested. "It hasn't even adjusted yet. Moving is a shock, you know."

Mrs. Cheetham looked genuinely ashamed. "I'm sorry," she said. "Of course you're right."

Charlotte couldn't believe Ruth would tell a scientist how to treat animals!

Ruth stuck her own finger through the cage. "Only I should touch him at first. That's what Mr. Johnson said. Soon I can train him to do all kinds of things. Mr. Johnson gave me a book. He said training this bird would be easy. It's the smartest bird he's had in months!"

Charlotte and Marie snickered at the same time. Leave it to Ruth to fall for a pitch like that. Look at this bird—it just sat there, all puffed up.

Their father gave both of them warning glances.

"What's its name?" Marie asked flatly, as if she didn't really care but supposed she had to know.

"Sam," Ruth said. "I've named him Sam."

Perfect, Charlotte thought. Just perfect. A dumb boring name for a dumb boring bird. And Ruth was beaming like she'd done the smartest thing on earth.

On Monday, Mrs. Sanchez stood at the front of the class and clasped her hands. She looked from face to face with a strange, meaningful smile. Where her gaze went, silence followed.

"My dears," she said quietly, when they'd all grown still. "I have something to announce. Something very wonderful. Our Charlotte"—she paused to beam at Charlotte—"has written us a very special play. A wonderful play. An *extraordinary* play! I mean a truly lively, lovely, little wonder of a play."

All heads turned. Charlotte felt a flush rising from the tip of her toes to her face. The play wasn't *that* good, and everyone knew it. Twenty sets of eyes stared. Charlotte frowned. It wasn't her fault Mrs. Sanchez got carried away.

The teacher reached behind her and pulled Charlotte's notebook from her desk. "This play is so full of fun," she continued. "So original."

Laura raised her hand. "What's it about?"

Mrs. Sanchez glowed. "It's about a silly little witch named Carlotta who can't help telling lies."

The class suddenly roared. Charlotte slid down in her seat and fought the urge to stick her head inside her desk.

"Gee," Tina muttered. "I seem to remember a witch like that!"

Mrs. Sanchez ignored everyone. Maybe she didn't know about Charlotte's lies and didn't get the joke. She was flipping happily through the play. "Carlotta tells all the other little witches at school that they needn't study chants," she went on enthusiastically. "All they have to do is use her new dot-me-magic that comes in tubes—lipstick, of course." She laughed aloud. "Oh, Charlotte, how clever!"

Now, when they should, no one laughed. Charlotte managed a feeble smile.

"And of course," Mrs. Sanchez continued, "the magic doesn't work. So when Morgan the Maniac tries to carry out his evil plot to lure innocent trick-or-treaters into his tent, the good little witches set out to stop him with useless dot-me-magic. With, of course, dreadful results. And—"

"There's a maniac?" Peter asked. He shot Charlotte his first friendly smile of the year.

Tina raised her hand.

Mrs. Sanchez peered across her glasses. She finally looked annoyed. "Yes, what is it?"

Tina lifted her chin. "If the dreadful results are death," she said, "forget it. Too violent."

Charlotte slid upright. *What?* Who was the one who'd wanted all the gory stuff in her novel last year? Who was the one who pushed everyone in school around all the time? Who was the meanest person in this class? Tina, that's who. She didn't care about violence one bit, except to use it!

29

"The results aren't death, Tina," Mrs. Sanchez said patiently. "But there *is* lots of suspense. Every good Halloween play needs that."

Peter waved his arm. "I want to be Morgan," he called.

Mrs. Sanchez sighed, her mood completely spoiled. Charlotte felt a wave of relief. If the teacher had kept raving on, the class would burn the play by lunch.

"It isn't the time to discuss all that," Mrs. Sanchez said in exasperation. She dropped the red notebook back onto the desk. "We audition for parts. Everyone will try out, and Charlotte and I will decide who's right."

Charlotte felt a buzzing in her ears. She didn't look at Annie.

"Obviously," Mrs. Sanchez went on, "we can't have twenty lead roles. And besides, a play is a joint venture. We all work together to make it good, so every part is important."

Peter frowned. "No it's not," he said. Across the room, Tina clearly agreed. She beamed with pleasure, imagining herself as the lead.

"I told you," Annie whispered on the way to lunch. "I *told* you you couldn't just pick parts."

Charlotte fumed. She was going to speak to Mrs. Sanchez about this. She hadn't even asked Charlotte's advice.

"It's fair, too," Annie pointed out. "No one can say you cheated."

Charlotte looked at Annie. Maybe she had a point. If Annie *was* best, the way Charlotte thought, then she could win an audition. And no one, even Tina, would be able to complain. That's how real art worked. You didn't make Tina the Great Grumble Witch just because you'd imagined her when you wrote—you only did it if she happened to fit the part. And if she happened to be the best Carlotta, then she got to be her. Charlotte swallowed hard. She couldn't imagine really letting Tina have the lead. Not even for art.

"That's true," Charlotte said. "When you win the audition it will be fair and square."

"I won't win," Annie said dully.

Charlotte turned her head so Annie wouldn't see her smile. Annie had just admitted it—she was going to try!

5

By Wednesday, Charlotte's play had multiplied into a tall stack of pages that sat on Mrs. Sanchez's desk. Charlotte stared at them in awe. Those were her words, typed up, copied, and stapled into twenty little books!

"I want you to take these home and read them as soon as possible," Mrs. Sanchez said as she handed each person a copy. "Give some thought to which parts you'd like to audition for. Maybe read the play with your friends and discuss who suits which role—how does that sound?"

"Dumb," Tina said under her breath. "We already know."

Mrs. Sanchez stopped. She looked at Tina. "Did you say something?" There was silence in the room. The teacher knew exactly what Tina had said.

"I said, 'Witchwork is *dumb.'* " Tina flashed her phoniest smile. It was one of Carlotta's lines, from the first page. Charlotte couldn't believe it. Tina thought she could get away with anything.

"Let's do our practicing at home," Mrs. Sanchez said coldly. "And I suggest those of you trying out for Carlotta also plan to try out for one or two other roles. There can be only one Carlotta, you know."

Behind the teacher's back, Tina pointed at herself and flashed a victory salute. Charlotte decided then and there: Art or no art, Tina would not get the lead.

"She really *is* a jerk," Annie agreed. They were walking home. Annie moved so slowly, Charlotte had to keep backing up. "But Laura could do it. I know she could. Laura would be great."

Charlotte didn't bother to reply. They both knew Laura was not going to audition for Carlotta against Tina. No one was, except Annie.

Annie slowed down even more. "I wouldn't mind it if I could act," she said. "I mean I'd *like* to beat Tina. I just never could in a million years."

Charlotte was getting fed up. Annie was wasting time. "Have you ever tried acting?" she demanded. "Even once?"

Annie blushed and shook her head.

"Just try," Charlotte insisted. "That's all I ask. Say 'Witchwork is dumb.' "

" 'Witchwork is dumb,' " Annie muttered.

"Louder!" Charlotte bellowed. " 'WITCH-WORK IS DUMB!' " She flung her book bag onto the ground. "Put some *feeling* into it!"

Annie backed off. "No!" she bellowed back. "I don't know how."

They stared at each other for a long, long time.

"Okay, Ruth." Mr. Cheetham banged on the bathroom door. "This has gone on long enough."

Charlotte and Marie stood close behind him. One person couldn't tie up the bathroom for hours. It was a family rule. Ruth was going to get it.

"I wanted to take a shower ages ago," Marie said. "I wanted to go out. I have things to do."

Charlotte nodded. She had things to do too. One of them was to find out what Ruth was doing every day in the bathroom.

The door opened and Ruth came out carrying a cardboard box. Her face was red with anger. "You scared him," she said to her father. "You almost scared him to death!"

Mr. Cheetham looked startled. "Scared who?"

"Sam!" Ruth brushed past them and headed down the hall toward her room, carrying the box carefully in front of her.

"Sam?" Mr. Cheetham exchanged bewildered looks with his younger daughters. "She had Sam in there?" he asked.

Charlotte was equally surprised. Did Sam take baths, or what? Maybe Ruth let him play in the sink. Wow.

"Ruth?" By the time the three of them had followed Ruth to her room, Sam was back in his cage. Ruth lay on her bed, sulking. "What were you doing in there?"

Ruth turned her face to the wall. "Training Sam," she said. "He's learning to walk up my arm and sit on my head. He lets me pet him now all the time. And I'm going to stick train him too!"

Charlotte didn't know what stick training was, but she was impressed. She'd never had a bird on her head.

"Really?" Mr. Cheetham looked impressed too. "In this short a time?"

Ruth nodded. Her face was still turned to the wall, but Charlotte could tell she had smiled.

"Well why in the bathroom?" Mr. Cheetham asked. "Why not in here, where there's more room to work?"

Ruth sat up. She swung her feet over the side of the bed. "My book says use a small space like a bathroom at first. And in there I can lock the door. I *have* to lock the door, or certain busybodies will open it up and he'll fly out." She glared at

36

Charlotte and Marie. "Then Pippi might get him."

"He flies around?" Mr. Cheetham said. He looked a little nervous at the thought.

"Well, of course." Ruth walked to the cage and peered in. "That's what birds *do*, isn't it? But I fix everything first. I cover the window and the mirror so he won't fly into them by mistake. And I put towels on the floor to cushion a fall. He likes it in there."

"Well, what do you know!" Mr. Cheetham laid a hand gently on Ruth's shoulder.

"There better not be bird doo in the tub," Marie said. "That's all I've got to say!" She stormed out of the room. Mr. Cheetham and Ruth exchanged amused looks.

Charlotte didn't like the looks one bit. Marie was right. There probably was bird doo all over the bathroom. Had anyone looked? And now that she thought about it, training a bird to sit on your head was a pretty dumb thing to do. One of these days Ruth would have bird doo there, too. Charlotte changed her mind: She wasn't impressed at all.

"Okay, class!" Mrs. Sanchez clapped her hands and waved her copy of the play in the air. "Have you been doing your reading? What do you think?"

"It's great!" Jenny said brightly.

"And funny!" someone else volunteered.

"Especially Great Grumble Witch of the Woods." Sarah Jacobson smiled at Charlotte. "I laughed every time I came to her."

Tina turned to look at Sarah like she was nuts. "She doesn't even have any lines," she pointed out. "She just grunts."

Sarah turned red. "Well, that's what's funny!"

Tina rolled her eyes and slid back around.

"There's only one bad thing," George said seriously. "There's not enough good parts for boys. If you're not Morgan the Maniac or his assistant, there's only homeowners or dumb little trick-or-treaters. And the assistant hardly has any lines. It's not fair, because there are more boys than girls in the class."

He was right, Charlotte realized. She should have had at least one other good boy's part. A policeman, or something like that. Maybe she could add it in.

"Those roles are perfectly good ones, George," Mrs. Sanchez said. "Two of the trick-or-treaters have a great deal to say, and the assistant has to ham it up looking evil, you know. I suspect your male ego is getting in the way here."

Charlotte felt sorry for George, but she was relieved. She didn't really have time to change

38

the play. It was going to take all her strength to turn Annie into a star.

"I'd like to remind everyone," Mrs. Sanchez went on, "that you won't all have major roles. That's just the way it is. Some of you, in fact, will only work props."

"I'd rather work props than have to grunt," Tina said loudly. "I would *never* take a role like that."

Mrs. Sanchez folded her arms and stared down at her. "Actually, Tina," she said finally, "I'm beginning to think the Great Grumble Witch role might suit you just fine."

Everyone laughed. Charlotte stared at Mrs. Sanchez. She couldn't believe it! It had taken six years, but it had finally happened: A teacher had come along who didn't like Tina!

Tina folded her own arms in reply and sulked.

"Now enough with complaints," Mrs. Sanchez said firmly. "Be prepared. Tomorrow is sign-up day."

6

Charlotte sat at her desk and frowned into her books. She couldn't concentrate on homework. She couldn't concentrate on anything. What if Annie didn't do it? What if no one but Tina signed up for Carlotta? Tina got everything and now she'd get this too, without even any work. It made Charlotte sick!

Hey, what was that noise? Charlotte paused in her sulking to listen. It was a scraping sound somewhere nearby. It sounded like mice, or rats inside the walls. Charlotte pushed back her chair. She bet anything it was rats! Good thing they had a cat.

She traced the sound into the hallway, where she found Pippi, clawing frantically at Ruth's door. She paused when she saw Charlotte, her eyes wide and her ears flat against her head. She wore what Charlotte's dad called her "insane look," the one that meant someone was driving her crazy. The someone was usually Mr. Cheetham, who made squeaky noises behind her back. Pippi loved being insane. She'd stand very still and then run off, but she always came slinking back for more.

"It's just a bird," Charlotte said grumpily. Pippi ignored her and went back to clawing. How had she known Sam was in there, anyway? He wasn't making a peep. "He's not even a pretty one," Charlotte added. "Or smart. He hasn't sung once."

At that moment Sam broke into song. Pippi's clawing grew wild. Sam's vibrating melody pierced the air and floated along the hallway. Charlotte held her breath. One little bird could make that beautiful sound? She stayed very still, to listen.

But there was Pippi, scratching like a maniac at the door. Suddenly *her* pet seemed like the dumb one. Charlotte snatched up the cat and carried her off, the song sailing along behind them. It was the loveliest, sweetest thing Charlotte had ever heard.

At the far end of the hall, Pippi wriggled out of Charlotte's arms and hurried back to the door.

Charlotte let her go. Pippi could scratch all day, but it wouldn't stop Sam. Charlotte closed her eyes to listen. Any minute now, Ruth would come home and brag and spoil the whole thing. Charlotte had to love Sam now, while she had the chance.

"Sam sings!" Ruth said happily at breakfast.

"We know, we know!" Marie rolled her eyes.

"Isn't it pretty?" Ruth insisted. "Isn't it the prettiest singing you've ever heard from a bird?"

Charlotte snorted. As if Ruth had ever listened to a bird in her whole life!

"It really is quite extraordinary," Mrs. Cheetham agreed. "Sam must be very happy in your room." Ruth glowed.

"Maybe I'll get a bird," Marie said. "It could be friends with Sam."

Ruth's glow dimmed. She narrowed her eyes. "Sam doesn't want a friend," she said. "He's happy by himself. You're just copying me."

"Sam *definitely* does not want a friend," Mrs. Cheetham said loudly.

"Oh, well, that's fair!" Marie pushed back her chair. "So now Ruth and Charlotte can have pets, but I can't!" She rushed from the room, forgetting to turn her toes out as she ran.

Upstairs, Sam began to sing. Pippi jumped

from the window ledge and rushed toward the steps.

"This bird is trouble," Charlotte said happily. "I've said so all along."

Mrs. Sanchez had placed a sign-up sheet on the table by the door. "Now, you won't all get your first-choice roles," she reminded them again. "So sign up for two or three. You need a good backup that you'll be happy with."

"Not me!" Tina announced. "I'm not being some wimpy little witch or a grunting pig. If I can't be Carlotta, forget it."

Mrs. Sanchez glowered at her. "Fine," she said abruptly. "If you don't get the role, you'll work props. Understood?"

Tina nodded. She wasn't worried.

During free time, everyone hovered over the sheet. George and Peter and Robert and Frank and Charles all signed up for Morgan. Tina signed up for Carlotta.

"Oh, come on girls," Mrs. Sanchez said, looking over the list. "There must be a few of you who'd like the lead. And Annie, you haven't signed up at all. Come on up here, dear."

Annie walked reluctantly to the front of the room. She didn't look at Mrs. Sanchez. She didn't look at Charlotte, who was holding the pen. She didn't look at the sign-up sheet.

Charlotte handed her the pen and tried to ESP a message through it: DO IT!

Annie wrote her name next to Great Grumble Witch. She laid down the pen.

"Oh, not just that, dear," Mrs. Sanchez said with disappointment. "Sign up for a speaking role too."

Annie shook her head.

Charlotte clenched her fists. She would never forgive Annie for this. Never! She wasn't even going to try. She wasn't even going to write her name on a dumb sheet of paper saying she *might* try.

"She'll do it," Charlotte said. Mrs. Sanchez looked surprised. Annie looked up and frowned. "She wants to be Carlotta. She'd *love* to be Carlotta!" Charlotte stopped. She hadn't planned to say just that. Annie was a deep dark shade of red.

"Really, Annie?" Mrs. Sanchez looked thrilled. "Oh, how lovely! Annie as Carlotta. I can see it now!"

Instantly the class grew still. *Annie as Carlotta?* That's what they were thinking.

It was Tina's laugh that broke the silence. She laughed harder and harder, pounding on her desk as if this were just too funny for words. Peter and Frank laughed too. A current of giggles began to ripple across the room.

Annie spun around and looked at them. Tina covered her mouth and pretended to try to stop laughing, but she bounced her shoulders even more. It was disgusting and mean.

Annie turned back to the table. She picked up the pen. Very carefully, in neat, bold print, she wrote down her name. Right next to Tina's.

7

"This ought to be good," Tina snickered at lunch. She pretended to whisper, but she wanted Charlotte and Annie to hear.

Charlotte heard. She knew what she meant, too: Annie couldn't do it in a million years. At this particular moment, Charlotte agreed. If Annie shrank up any smaller, she'd disappear.

"You have to *act* like a star," Charlotte said when they were on the playground. Annie was sulking over the spectacle of Tina, reciting Charlotte's lines to a crowd. "Look at that. If you *act* like a star, you'll be one."

Annie kicked halfheartedly at a stone. "Well, if I *were* a star, I wouldn't have to act," she said. She gave a sudden ferocious kick and the stone scudded across the playground into the wall.

46

"That's it!" Charlotte said encouragingly. "That's the way stars act!"

Annie stood very still and widened her eyes as far as they'd go. It was exactly like Pippi's insane look.

"We should practice," Charlotte said on the way home. "You read lines and I'll direct."

Annie shook her head.

"Annie, you have to practice! Auditions are *soon!*"

Annie hid her face behind her books. "I can't believe you made me do it, Charlotte!" Her voice was a muffled mix of misery and disbelief. "You know I can't beat Tina!"

Charlotte sighed. "Yes, you can. Look, you have the director helping you out. Does Tina have that? And the teacher *wants* you to win. She practically said it!"

Annie didn't look reassured. She lowered her books and stared straight ahead. "It was a mistake. I'm going to tell Mrs. Sanchez that. I signed up by mistake, because you tricked me into it."

Charlotte started counting slowly to ten. She only made it to four. "Fine!" she exploded. "We'll just *give* this play to Tina. Tina who is a rat and a show-off and the most obnoxious person we know. Tina who laughed at you all day. Tina,

47

WHO WILL GET WHAT SHE'S WANTED SINCE THE FIRST GRADE!" Charlotte's voice had grown louder with every word. Now she was shouting. "LET'S JUST DO THAT!"

Annie was going to cry. Well, good. She *should* feel bad. She was about to ruin her whole future and spoil the play.

"And all because you won't try." Charlotte gave her head a sad little shake. "I mean, if you couldn't do it, that would be one thing. But you can. You just won't *try*."

A tear rolled down Annie's cheek. She brushed it angrily away.

"I have too tried, Charlotte," she said. "I try at home. I practically know Carlotta's lines by heart."

Charlotte stopped walking. She stared hopefully at her friend. *"Really?"*

Annie's eyes were watery and strangely bright. She nodded. "I say them to myself. All the time."

"Well, how do they sound?" Charlotte asked eagerly. "Are you any good?"

Annie gave an embarrassed little laugh. "I don't know. I only say them in my head. Never out loud. I'm afraid."

"Well, pretend you're saying them to yourself, but say them out loud. It's the same thing."

Annie frowned. "No it isn't. Words sound different in the air than they do in your head."

They did? This was news to Charlotte. But then her words didn't spend much time in her head. They always popped right out of her mouth. It was her greatest fault. It was why she used to lie when she hadn't planned to at all. There wasn't enough time to stop herself.

"But I guess I could try," Annie said quietly. "Just once."

"Oh! That singing is beautiful." Annie stood, transfixed, in the hallway listening to Sam. She had Pippi locked in her arms. Pippi squirmed.

"Bring that cat in here, fast," Charlotte commanded, moving ahead into the bedroom. She shut the door behind them. "She hates Sam."

"Really?" Annie sat on the bed and gathered Pippi into a ball on her lap. One by one, she petted Pippi's favorite spots. Pippi lifted her chin and tipped her head to make it easy.

"Of course," Charlotte said. "Wouldn't you? The first thing everyone does when they get home is run to see Sam and rave about him. 'Oh, look, Sam is swinging.' 'Oh, look, Sam is eating.' Big deal, you know?"

"Sam swings?" Annie looked interested. "You mean he just sits there and swings himself back and forth like a kid?"

Charlotte sighed. "Yes, he swings."

"Cute. What else does he do?" Annie continued to rub under Pippi's chin. Charlotte thought it was pretty hypocritical to be asking about one pet while you were holding another. She wasn't going to say so, though. She needed Annie in a good mood.

"Nothing much. Bird stuff. Now, what should we read?" She thumbed through the play searching for an exciting part. If it was exciting, Annie might get worked up without thinking about it. "Here," she said. "Let's read this—where Carlotta tells the big lie. I'll be Little Witch One."

Annie looked like someone about to be hanged. She sat up very straight on the bed. Pippi wandered off her lap to the pillow and settled in for a nap.

" 'Oh, Carlotta,' " Charlotte read. " 'How do you ever expect to pass if you don't do witchwork at night? You won't know your chants and spells!' "

Annie swallowed hard. " 'I don't have to do witchwork,' " she said in a flat voice. " 'I have flair.' "

Charlotte stared at her. If ever somebody didn't have flair, it was the Carlotta sitting on the bed. "Annie! That's not acting!"

Annie blushed.

"Look." Charlotte draped herself across the armchair in the corner of the room. She lifted her

nose and studied her nails. " 'I have flair-r-r,' "
she drawled. " 'Darlings, I have flair-r-r.' " She
sprang up in excitement and rushed to her desk.
"Yes," she said, penciling a note in the margin
of the page. " 'Darlings' is good. She should say
'darlings' whenever she talks to the other little
witches. It's so—pompous, you know?" Pompous was one of her favorite words lately. It was
such a perfect description of Ruth. Tina too.
"Okay. Now you say it."

Annie continued to sit bolt upright. " 'Darlings,' " she whispered. " 'I have flair.' " She
squeezed her eyes closed and then opened them
very slowly. She and Charlotte looked at each
other.

"Louder," Charlotte whispered back. Annie
was about to do it, Charlotte could tell.

" 'Darlings,' " Annie said, still staring into
Charlotte's eyes. " 'I have flair!' " It was a little
louder and more enthusiastic.

"Again," Charlotte ordered. She had the funny
feeling Annie was taking energy from *her*, as if
Charlotte had hypnotized her, or something.

Annie stood up. She put her hands on her hips
and raised her head.

" 'Dah-lings,' " she drawled perfectly, " 'I
have flair-r-r!' "

Charlotte jumped up, her chair crashing behind

51

her. "That's it, Annie!" She shook her friend by the shoulders. "That's it!"

Annie's hands dropped from her hips and her mouth fell open. "It is?" she said in surprise. She slowly began to smile. "Wow," she said quietly. "Weird."

8

"I can't decide about Carlotta's hair," Tina said loudly. "Orange curls or green streaks. Which do you think?"

Laura looked thoughtful. "Green streaks. Carlotta would be sort of wild like that."

"But orange curls might be her natural hair," Jenny said. "Halloween-y."

Charlotte frowned. Carlotta's hair would be whatever color Charlotte decided to make it, and she hadn't decided yet. She didn't comment, though. Tina was just trying to make her mad.

In the center of the classroom, Peter stood on his head. He kicked his feet. He "ya-hooed" and crashed to the floor. He was working on being more of a maniac than George or Charles. George and Charles were good, though. George was chuckling and stuffing imaginary body parts into

53

a paper bag, while Charles shot at invisible pumpkins, splashing them to bits.

" 'Dot me here, dot me there, dot me, dot me, everywhere!' " sang three Little Witch Ones. Mrs. Sanchez had given them five more minutes to practice before each one had to stand in front of the class and do something. Warm-up exercises, Mrs. Sanchez called them. Auditions were only one week away.

"Okay, everyone," she said when the fifteen minutes were up. "Settle down. Take out your copies of the play. I'm going to call you up here one by one, and you can read any part you choose for two minutes. Peter, you first."

Peter strode to the front of the room. "I'll read Morgan," he announced. Everyone laughed. As if they didn't know!

" 'Okay, you stupid little trick-or-treaters,' " he read. He talked like that movie star in the old movies who spoke from the side of his mouth. " 'Welcome to the Tent of Treats!' " He cackled and gestured toward the imaginary tent. " 'Come and get your biggest treat of all!' " Trick-or-treaters who went into that tent never came out. Peter made it seem real and scary. He just might win, Charlotte thought as she watched. When he tricked his first victim into the tent he wiggled his eyebrows at the audience and everyone laughed. She didn't *like* Peter, but she was willing to forget it if he was best for the part.

Mrs. Sanchez nodded when his time was up. "Excellent, Peter. All right. Who's next?"

Lots of people waved their hands, but the teacher ignored them. She called on Annie.

"Me?" Annie squeaked. She fidgeted lamely with her script.

"Yes, dear," Mrs. Sanchez said kindly. "I'd like you to read Carlotta. Loudly and clearly."

Annie walked slowly to the front of the class. She turned and looked out. The color drained from her face. Charlotte's heart gave a terrified lurch. Annie was going to blow it! And if she blew it now, she'd never try again!

" 'I don't have to do witchwork,' " Annie was saying dully. She didn't look at her script. She didn't look at the class. She seemed to be dazed. " 'I have flair.' " She sounded like a robot reciting lines.

Everyone laughed at the robot with flair. Charlotte glared around the room. Annie *did* have flair. She *did!* If they'd just wait a minute, they'd see.

But Annie wasn't going to show them. Already she was sliding back into her seat. Charlotte dropped her head onto her arms and moaned.

Annie cried all the way home. "I told you, Charlotte," she sobbed. "I *told* you!"

Charlotte trudged guiltily along behind. Why had she made Annie do it? Why had she tried to make her a star when Annie didn't want to be one? What kind of friend did a thing like that?

"You can quit, Annie," Charlotte said. "Really. I don't mind. If you don't want to be Carlotta, you don't have to be. You don't even have to be in the play. You can draw scenery. You're great in art."

Annie stopped abruptly and turned around. Beneath her glasses, her eyes were swollen and red. "I don't *want* to draw scenery," she said fiercely. "I want to be Carlotta! I want that more than anything else!"

Charlotte didn't know what to say. Annie had been awful today. Worse than awful. She could never be Carlotta now. Why would she want to try?

"I know," Annie hiccuped miserably. "I stank. And I'll never get the lead. But now I'm going to want it for the rest of my life!"

When Annie left, a big hole seemed to open up in the space where she'd been. An empty hole with no air. Charlotte couldn't breathe. This was all her fault. She had ruined the rest of her best friend's life.

9

"Mr. Bergen says I can do my science report on Sam," Ruth said at dinner. "Birds as domestic pets."

Big deal. Charlotte leaned her chin in her hand and chewed. Her play—her wonderful play— was going to have Peter and Tina as the leads. Tina had been good at her reading. She'd yelled and stomped around the stage having flair. So now they'd have to pick her.

"I must admit Sam's a fascinating bird," Mr. Cheetham said.

Charlotte sat up. What was fascinating about Sam? He only sang and ate.

"You know what he does now?" Ruth said enthusiastically. "When I hang up one of those little seed bells, he eats what he wants and then pecks the wire till it breaks and crashes to the floor. It's his way of saying he's done, because he won't go near his floor."

"Well who would?" Charlotte wrinkled her nose. All that bird you-know-what all over the place!

"Sounds wasteful to me," Mrs. Cheetham said.

Ruth scowled. "It's cute. And interesting. Scientifically."

Mrs. Cheetham, the scientist, smiled. "Yes," she agreed, "I suppose it is."

Charlotte grunted to herself. Now *Pippi* was cute. And interesting. Scientifically. She'd chewed a phone cord in half. And sucked all those little holes in Charlotte's blanket. She did interesting things all day long. Whenever Mr. Cheetham opened his newspaper to read, didn't Pippi climb onto his lap and squish it flat? *Every time.* Pippi was always climbing and jumping into trouble. Once she'd leaped onto the toilet when the lid and the seat were both up and fallen right in. What could a bird do compared to that? Mr. Bergen was a pushover.

Charlotte was supposed to be at school early the next day to discuss scenery. She wished Annie would come, but she was afraid to ask. The very word "scenery" made Annie scowl.

Charlotte trudged to school alone. She wondered if Annie would show up at all. She didn't think *she* would, if she were Annie. She'd want the class to have as many days as they could to forget.

Mrs. Sanchez was bustling around the room as usual, hanging up posters they'd made in art. "Cheery spaces make cheery faces," she liked to say. Peter always stuck his finger down his throat when she said it.

"Good morning, dear," she said brightly to Charlotte. She stood back to admire a poster, then brushed her hands together. "Isn't that nice? It's one of Annie's." The picture had flower pots all in a row. Charlotte couldn't bear to look at it. Annie had made it when she was happy.

"Charlotte? Is something wrong?"

Charlotte took a deep breath. "I guess we'll have to give Tina the lead," she blurted out. There, she'd said it. She'd done the thing that was fair.

Mrs. Sanchez looked surprised. "Why do you say that? Because of yesterday?"

Of course because of yesterday. "Yes!" Charlotte said. "Annie was awful. You saw how she did."

"But it wasn't the real audition," Mrs. Sanchez said thoughtfully. "I think Annie was just a little nervous, don't you?"

Charlotte nodded eagerly. "She was! She's

really good when we practice at home." The last time they'd practiced, Annie had stomped her foot three times and not even known she'd done it.

"Great!" Mrs. Sanchez looked pleased. "If she can do it at home, she can do it at school."

Charlotte wasn't so sure. It would take a miracle to bring Annie's confidence back now. "We have to make her better than Tina," she reminded the teacher.

"Oh, pooh." Mrs. Sanchez dismissed Tina with a wave of the hand. "Tina's bold. She makes a lot of noise. But that's not acting. I think maybe Annie could *act*."

A little chill ran along Charlotte's spine. It was true! Tina was only noise, and Annie could act! Charlotte had known the difference. She just hadn't known how to say it.

"Why don't you girls go to the library," Mrs. Sanchez suggested. "See what books are available on acting. I think if Annie studies a bit, with your help she might pull it off."

Charlotte stared. She couldn't believe how Mrs. Sanchez understood things. Last year she'd known Charlotte could write a play before Charlotte had even tried. Now she knew Annie could act when she hadn't seen her do it. She even knew that inside of perfect know-it-all Tina there was a great big rat, though of course she couldn't say it.

"You're right," Charlotte said. She believed it, too.

"The library?" Annie looked doubtful. They were seated on the little stone wall that surrounded the playground while everyone else ate lunch inside. Annie wouldn't sit at that table with those kids and Charlotte didn't blame her. All morning Peter kept asking to see a little flair. What a jerk!

Charlotte nodded. "Mrs. Sanchez said there are books about acting. And she said she knew you could act. You just need a little help. Lots of real actors are shy. Mrs. Sanchez said that in person they're usually nothing like they are onstage."

"Well in person I'm *just* like I am onstage!"
Charlotte sighed.

Annie's eyes flashed. "You know it too, Charlotte! Even you said I should draw scenery instead."

Charlotte stood up. "I did not! I said if you didn't want to *act*, you should draw scenery. Then you said you *did* want to act. You said you wanted it more than anything in your whole life!"

Annie looked embarrassed. She grinned. "Well, I do!"

Charlotte grabbed hold of Annie's arm and pulled her off the wall. "Then let's go!" Honestly! Some best friends could drive you nuts.

"Books on acting?" Mrs. Arnold, the librarian, smiled. "Does this mean you've finished your play?"

Charlotte nodded happily. Mrs. Arnold would love the play. She knew how hard Charlotte had worked to make it a thing of beauty. Charlotte had thought about the librarian the whole time she wrote. She'd put in all those parts about the full moon and round orange pumpkins and falling leaves because Mrs. Arnold said good writing could make you *feel* places. Charlotte was going to have leaves dumped onstage and all around the audience so they'd crunch when you walked.

"I think you'll like it," Charlotte said. "Even my dad said it's good. A thing of beauty, and all that." She blushed. She supposed she shouldn't brag. She just wanted Mrs. Arnold to know she'd done something right for a change.

"Wonderful!" The librarian beamed. "I can't wait to see it. Who has the lead?"

Charlotte and Annie looked at each other. Annie looked away. She studied a row of nearby books.

"Annie might," Charlotte said. "We're having tryouts soon."

Mrs. Arnold nodded thoughtfully. "So you want books for Annie. Hm-m-m." She seemed to scan the bookshelves in her mind. Charlotte bet she knew the location of every single book in this room. They were like children to her. When you checked them out, she expected you to treat them with respect. Charlotte had always liked to think how someday her own books would sit here with the rest of Mrs. Arnold's kids and be loved.

"I know!" Mrs. Arnold hurried to the wall behind her desk. It was where she kept the special books only teachers could use. "I have the perfect thing." She pulled down one book and then another. "Here. These are really written for teachers, but I think they'd be a big help to you. And they seldom get used."

Charlotte examined them. One was called *A Teacher's Guide to Putting On a Play* and the other was *The Art of the Actor*. Perfect! There was one for each of them.

"These are great," Charlotte said. "Thanks."

"Yes," Annie mumbled. Her face looked like a round orange pumpkin with a smile painted on. "Thanks."

10

Charlotte and Annie sat on the bedroom floor. Annie held her book open on her lap, but she hadn't turned a page once.

"Read," Charlotte commanded.

Annie shot her a look, but she turned a page.

Charlotte wasn't exactly thrilled with her own book. The opening paragraph said, "School plays can be, and usually are, agonizing experiences. Young students may lack interest, dramatic skill, and even the slightest technical knowledge of stage performance." If you asked Charlotte, it was a dumb way to start a book on plays. Any normal person would just decide not to have one.

The second paragraph cheered her up a bit. It explained that by reading this book you could be prepared for all those things that might go wrong. This book was thick, though. It would take her till Halloween just to read it.

"How's your book?" Charlotte asked after a while. Maybe she didn't have to read this one. Really, it was Annie who needed help. Mrs. Sanchez had been putting on plays for years. If any agonizing experiences were going to come along, she'd know how to deal with them.

"Fine," Annie said unenthusiastically. Her chin was propped in her hand. She turned another page.

Charlotte skipped to Chapter Two. "Organizing Your Director's Book," it was called. This sounded a little more interesting. "Keep a notebook," the first paragraph advised. Charlotte would love to do that. She'd use her new purple Trapper-Keeper with the folders inside. You were supposed to write down ideas about costumes and scenery and make schedules for rehearsals. You could even keep a copy of the play in the book and make notes in the margin as you went along about the mood each scene should have. Charlotte slammed her book shut and went to fetch her notebook. She'd read enough. She had work to do.

Annie slammed her book too.

"You read," Charlotte said irritably, searching through the junk piled on her shelves. As she recalled, she'd left this stuff in perfect order on the floor. Her mother had been organizing again, messing things up. It drove Charlotte crazy. She found her notebook and pulled it out.

"But I don't get this," Annie complained. She flung her book aside. "It talks about energy points and thinking like a nose."

Thinking like a *nose*? Charlotte picked up Annie's book and opened it. "One method encourages actors to focus their powers of concentration so that energy is harnessed for theatrical use," she read. Yuck. Annie's opening page was worse than hers. She skimmed it, looking for the thinking nose.

"Let's just forget it, Charlotte." Annie pulled the book out of Charlotte's hands. "Tina's going to win. You know she is. Even if I were good— even if I were *great*, I wouldn't be as good as her. She's already great, and she has the same amount of time to get better."

"She's not great!" Charlotte spread her notebook open on the floor. DIRECTOR'S BOOK she wrote in giant green letters on the first piece of paper. "She's loud. That's what Mrs. Sanchez said. Just loud."

Annie giggled. "Mrs. Sanchez said that?"

"Yep." Charlotte turned to page two. PROPS, she wrote at the top. "She said just being loud was not acting, either."

Annie nodded. "She's right," she agreed.

"Like when Tina said, 'Witchwork is dumb!' She didn't put any feeling into it. She just yelled."

"Yeah. You have to make it *real*. Like you *think* witchwork is dumb." Charlotte turned the page. COSTUMES, she wrote at the top.

Annie rolled over and sat up. " 'Witchwork is dumb!' " she said. It sounded right. Like she meant it. She met Charlotte's eyes for the first time all day. "Like that."

Excitement roared through Charlotte but she didn't say a word. She didn't want to scare Annie now. She nodded as calmly as she could.

"Maybe Mrs. Arnold would help me read the book," Annie added eagerly.

Charlotte sat up. "Or my dad!" Her dad knew about all creative things and he loved to be asked for advice—as long as you didn't interrupt his work, of course.

"Do you think he would?" Annie asked. "He wouldn't mind?"

Charlotte shook her head. He definitely would not mind. He was wandering around upstairs, not even near his easel.

He didn't mind, either. He sat on Charlotte's bed and thumbed through the book with interest. "Of course you can act, Annie," he assured her. "You have spirit, and hidden depths."

"But very hidden," Charlotte explained. "She's shy."

68

Her father didn't look concerned. "She'll overcome it. Acting is an art. Any art has to be learned. That's why there are schools of acting. Master's degrees in drama. Stanislavsky. Ever hear of him?" He waved the book.

Charlotte sighed. "Dad, this play is on Halloween. Next month. There isn't time for Annie to get a master's degree."

Mr. Cheetham nodded. "So that's why I'm here," he said, spreading his arms. "To teach Ellis Cheetham's Crash Course One."

Charlotte and Annie looked at each other. Charlotte had a funny feeling that crash would be the right name for this course.

"Don't you do it!" Charlotte said warningly to Pippi, who'd been about to plop herself right down in the middle of Charlotte's Director's Book. Charlotte had worked on the book for hours. It was filled with ideas about coaching skills and costumes and props. She'd glued a production calendar to the front, just like the book she'd read suggested. Later she was going to put the script in there too, and make notes in the margin about the mood she wanted to develop in each scene. It was a lot of work, but it was worth it. This Director's Book was going to keep her play from being an agonizing experience.

"Charlotte?" Her mother stuck her head in the doorway. "What on earth are you doing? I've called you five times. Dinner!"

Her father winked when she joined them at the table. "Annie coming tomorrow?" he asked. The next day was Sunday. They were having the first meeting of Crash Course One.

Charlotte nodded and smiled. Annie had called four times today to be sure Mr. Cheetham hadn't changed his mind. Then she called twice because she'd changed hers.

"What's going on tomorrow?" Mrs. Cheetham asked. "Something fun?"

"Work." Mr. Cheetham looked very serious. "We're going to turn Annie into a star."

"Oh, my." Mrs. Cheetham smiled. "That *will* be work."

Both Charlotte and her father glared at her.

"It's no joke," Charlotte said. "Tryouts for my play are this week. We want Annie to get the lead."

Marie and Ruth laughed.

"It stars a mouse, right?" Ruth said.

"Ruth!" Mrs. Cheetham scowled at her, then looked at Charlotte with narrowed eyes. "How exactly do you plan to turn Annie into a star?" she asked. "I can't imagine she'd want to be one."

"She'll want to when she learns how to act,"

70

Charlotte said. "That's why we're having this course."

"*We?*" Mrs. Cheetham studied her husband. "You, I suppose, are Stanislavsky," she said in what Charlotte thought was a mean tone of voice. Mr. Cheetham suddenly looked meek.

"No," Charlotte said, "he's not. He's Ellis Cheetham of Crash Course One. That's even better!"

Mrs. Cheetham rolled her eyes.

11

Annie looked like a ghost who had floated into the studio and gotten stuck to the floor. Any moment now she would float up again and disappear.

"I think you both need to start out with a few basic exercises," Mr. Cheetham said, flipping through Annie's library book. "Who wants to go first?"

Annie didn't blink. Her mouth was a little "o." She looked dead, but with her mouth open.

"I'm the director," Charlotte pointed out. "I don't have to act."

Mr. Cheetham smiled mildy. "Acting skills are a must for any director," he said. "How else can you spot flaws in your performers?" He gave her a meaningful look. Charlotte got it: She was supposed to go first just to let Annie relax.

"Now." Mr. Cheetham propped the book on his easel. "Exercise one. Charlotte, you're walking a tightrope. It runs from the easel here to the table over there. Let's see you do it."

Charlotte felt ridiculous placing one foot in front of the other and waving her arms in the air. This wasn't *acting*. It was playing. She hoped her father knew what he was doing.

Her father nodded when she was done. "All right, now tell me—did you have a net under you?"

Charlotte blinked. "I don't know. You're the one who invented the tightrope. Did you invent a net?" She laughed and glanced at Annie. Annie's eyes, however, were riveted on Charlotte's dad.

"How high up were you?" he continued. "Was it your first time or your fifty-fifth? Were there people watching you or not? Did you get scared?"

Charlotte glared at her father. She hoped he wasn't going to get carried away and be like this all day. Annie was the one they were supposed to train. "I don't know," she said irritably.

Mr. Cheetham waved his pencil and motioned her to the chair by the door. "Then you didn't act," he said. "When you act, you know these things. You *feel* how high up in the air you are. You're conscious of the crowd. And certainly, if you're on a tightrope, you don't stare at your feet."

Charlotte was furious. How could you tell where to put your feet if you didn't look at them? And he hadn't told her to imagine a crowd. He'd just told her to *walk*. She plopped down in the chair. It felt like being sent to sit in a corner.

"Okay, Annie. Now you."

Annie moved slowly to the easel. She took a deep breath and closed her eyes. Poor Annie! Charlotte had never known her father could be so mean.

Suddenly Annie held out her arms. Slowly, carefully, she began to walk, swaying gently as she went. Once, she tilted, as if to fall. Charlotte gasped, it was so real. Annie went on. She didn't look like Annie at all. She looked like a person walking a rope in the air.

"Wonderful!" Mr. Cheetham said when she was done. Annie turned red and hurried to sit down. "Annie, you imagined it perfectly."

It was true, Charlotte admitted sullenly. But so could *she* have if she hadn't had to go first. Annie'd been able to learn from her mistakes.

"Now." Mr. Cheetham reached for the book and flipped a page. "You're riding a bus. Going downtown after school." He motioned Charlotte from the chair she was sitting on and plunked it into the center of the room. It was supposed to be the seat on the bus. "Okay, Charlotte. Here you go."

This time Charlotte knew what to do. She grunted and groaned and climbed the bus steps. It had been a hard day at school. She was so tired. And of course there was only one seat and it was on the other side of a gigantic woman with a million bags full of stuff. How could she ever squeeze past *her*? The woman didn't even move to let Charlotte by. Charlotte wiggled and squirmed. Ugh! Now she was smushed against the window in this tiny space and the woman wore too much perfume. Charlotte wrinkled her nose. Also, the woman's huge hat kept poking Charlotte in the eye. She could not *wait* to get off this bus. When her stop came, she had to squeeze by again because the woman wouldn't budge. She was so rude! Charlotte was exhausted by the time she finally got off. She wiped her forehead and sank beside Annie on the floor.

Annie and Mr. Cheetham stared.

"Well?" Charlotte said. "How'd I do?" She knew the answer, of course, but she wanted to hear them say it.

Her father and Annie looked at each other. They looked back, at her. *"What* did you do?" her father asked with a bewildered smile. "That was the liveliest bus ride I've ever seen."

"I was squished against the window!" Charlotte stood up. That had been obvious! "There was a giant woman with a million bags who wouldn't let me by. She was rude, and she smelled, too!" Where were their imaginations? Annie hadn't had to explain every move she made. "And she wore a hat that poked me in the eye. I couldn't breathe or see!"

Mr. Cheetham started to laugh. He laughed harder and harder, until his head fell onto his notebook, and he was just a round shaking mound. At that moment Charlotte hated her father. He was a disgusting man and a terrible teacher.

Charlotte looked at Annie, daring her to laugh. Annie was staring off into space, biting her lips.

When it was Annie's turn, she did a boring little ride where nothing happened. She put her money in the box and took her seat. She smiled at the people around her and looked out the window. Right before she got off, she reached up and pulled the cord. Big deal. It was the dullest thing Charlotte had ever seen in her entire life.

"There are no tightropes or buses in the Halloween play," she announced. "This is a big waste of time."

Her father chuckled and wiped a leftover tear from his eye. "No it isn't," he said. "You're just not taking it seriously enough."

She wasn't taking it seriously enough? *She* wasn't taking it seriously? Who was the one doing all the laughing here? She wondered if her father was this obnoxious when he taught art at the university. Good thing Mrs. Cheetham made lots of money. Mr. Cheetham was going to be fired any day.

"You were right, Charlotte," he said after Annie left. He was so excited his face glowed. "Annie can act. I mean *really* act."

Charlotte didn't reply. She was too mad. But still, he *had* gotten Annie to act, even if he'd done it in a dumb way. For a while, she supposed, she'd have to let him be obnoxious.

12

Charlotte pulled out her Director's Book. "Have actors practice walking tightropes," she wrote down under COACHING SKILLS. Tina would be terrible at that. She'd stomp across the floor like a horse.

From down the hall came the sound of Ruth and Marie, arguing. Charlotte sighed. You could never get work done in this house. She hurried to Ruth's room to find out what this one was about.

"That's the dumbest thing I ever heard," Marie was saying. She and Ruth bent close to Sam's cage. "Birds do not have tongues."

Ruth straightened up and folded her arms. "They most certainly do. I've seen Sam's. And how would you know? I'm the one who knows about birds. I'm doing my report on them."

"Okay then," Marie said with a smirk. "Did you ever see a bird stick out its tongue?"

They all looked at Sam. Charlotte smiled. If ever a bird were going to stick out its tongue, now would be the time to do it. Sam, however, merely looked bored.

"Just because they don't stick it out, doesn't mean they don't have one," Ruth argued.

Charlotte thought she had a point. She studied Sam curiously. *Did* birds have tongues? The feathers on his head puffed out when she leaned close. He was awfully cute. And day by day his orange cheeks seemed to get a little brighter, like Ruth kept saying they would.

Sam suddenly hopped back and forth on his swing. "Meow," he said.

Everyone stared. "Meow," Sam repeated. "Meow, meow, meow!" Ruth and Marie stepped back from the cage in alarm.

Charlotte, however, didn't move. She knew exactly what was going on. Most birds copied people because it was people they heard. This bird heard a cat meowing all day long at his door, so he copied that. He wasn't afraid of Pippi one bit—he'd turned her into a song!

"Oh, my God!" Ruth said. She clapped her hand over her mouth. "A bird that meows! I don't believe it."

Charlotte didn't believe it either. Ruth had gotten a wonderful bird. A *great* bird. A bird with flair. It should never have happened. Not to Ruth. It should have happened to her.

"Now when you get up there, just do what my father said," Charlotte told Annie on Monday morning. There was going to be this one day of read-throughs before the real auditions later this week. "Forget where you are. Imagine you're Carlotta." It wouldn't even matter if she wasn't very good. Today she had to work on just getting her nerve. At the audition she could *act*.

Mrs. Sanchez gave Charlotte a little wink when she called on Annie. She was sure Annie would be good. Charlotte crossed all the toes and fingers she could.

Annie stared out at the class, just as she had before. She mumbled her words, just as she had before.

"Look!" Peter yelled. "Flair!"

Tina laughed.

"Stop it!" Mrs. Sanchez said angrily. "Never mind, Annie. You just practice a little more." She patted Annie kindly on the back, but Charlotte could see that Mrs. Sanchez was disappointed. And she wouldn't look at Charlotte. Charlotte could tell by her face that she didn't really believe in Annie anymore.

If only she'd brought her Director's Book to show how acting took skill. Annie had skill. If the class had to do all the exercises in the book, they would know.

"We should walk tightropes!" Charlotte hollered.

There was silence in the room. They stared at her like she was nuts. Even Mrs. Sanchez.

"Tightropes, Charlotte?" she said.

Charlotte's ears began to burn. "It's an acting exercise," she explained. "Where you pretend to walk a rope across the room. Or we could do riding a bus."

Mrs. Sanchez sighed and turned away. "I think we'd better practice reading the script," she said wearily. "We're having enough trouble with that." Across the room, Annie turned her face to the wall.

"It was really that bad?" her father said with a worried frown.

Charlotte nodded. "Worse! And Annie won't even talk. She didn't say one word all the way home. Auditions are tomorrow, Dad! Mrs. Sanchez said we'd fooled around long enough. She's given up on Annie, I can tell, and Annie knows it, too."

"Get her over here." Mr. Cheetham threw down his paper.

Now? Charlotte looked at the clock. It was eight thirty on a school night. Annie wouldn't be allowed out.

"Better yet, we'll go to her. Call her mother and see if it's okay."

Mrs. Block sounded surprised, but she agreed.

Annie answered the door. She looked from one to the other with a zombielike face. Charlotte felt like an attack team.

"Crash Course Two," Mr. Cheetham announced. He marched into the living room. "How to Forget Your Audience."

Annie stood there with the door wide open.

"Come on," Mr. Cheetham called. He shoved a footstool out of the center of the room and motioned for Annie to take its place. "You're going to learn to block us out." He maneuvered himself and Charlotte to the sofa. "Should be easy for someone whose name is Annie Block." He smiled at Annie over his shoulder.

Annie didn't smile back. She still hadn't moved. Mr. Cheetham returned and gently steered her to the center of the room.

"Let me tell you something," he said, sitting down on the sofa. He sat close to the edge so he could pop up again if he had to. Charlotte could *feel* his energy in the air. "All artists have to find their own space. They have to find it and protect it and keep everyone else outside it."

Annie looked as if a flea flying into her could knock her out of *her* space.

"Take me for instance." Mr. Cheetham tapped on his chest. "When I'm painting a picture, I'm not aware of anything else that's going on." Charlotte nodded. She could agree to that. "I'm completely absorbed in what I'm doing. There's the object I want to paint, and there's the canvas I'm going to paint it on. I study the object. I think about it. I imagine it on the canvas. I start to paint. No! That's not the way it looks. I start again. I mix my paints. I rearrange the object. I paint again. There—that's better. Do you see what I mean? It's just me, the object, the canvas, the paint."

Annie shifted her feet. She looked at Charlotte. She looked at the door, considering escape.

Mr. Cheetham didn't notice. "And take Charlotte Shakespeare here," he continued. "When she was writing this play, we would call her to dinner a hundred times and she wouldn't hear. She was busy imagining, and when you imagine, you live in that imaginary world for a while. You live in that world and you forget this one. You block it out."

Annie suddenly looked interested. Charlotte knew there were lots of times Annie would like to forget this world. It wasn't always so nice to her. "Yes," Annie said slowly. "You know, when I

84

was walking that tightrope, I forgot where I was!"

Mr. Cheetham beamed. "Because you were imagining so well! Because you're an artist, Annie. I know it."

But Annie had wilted again. "I can't do it in front of people though," she said unhappily. "Not at school."

Mr. Cheetham laughed. "If you're an actor, in front of people is the only place you *can* do it," he said. "How do you block out an audience that isn't there?"

Charlotte studied her father in awe. He really was a genius. And it wasn't just something she thought because he was her dad.

"It's all a question of preparing yourself ahead of time. Before school tomorrow, start imagining you're Carlotta. Start thinking like her and feeling like her and acting like her. See the kids as characters in the play. That way, when it's time to audition, you can just step right into the scene."

"Do actors do that?" Charlotte asked curiously. It sounded like fun. Maybe she should change careers.

"Sure." Her father smiled. "That's what makes them so hard to live with. There are actors who stay in character the whole time they're making a movie."

Annie suddenly giggled. "I'm glad I'm not married to Rambo," she said.

Mr. Cheetham laughed. He sat back, wiggling comfortably into a corner of the sofa. He thought he'd done it, Charlotte knew. He thought his one little talk had changed Annie's personality forever. He hadn't been there today. *Maybe* Annie could do it. Maybe not.

"You know what?" Annie said shyly. Her voice was quiet, but Charlotte could hear a tiny bit of excitement underneath the fear.

"What?" Mr. Cheetham asked.

"My mother told me last night that she used to act. When she was in high school, she had the lead in *Romeo and Juliet*."

"Really?" Mr. Cheetham raised his eyebrows. "And you never knew?"

Annie shook her head.

"Well there, you see!" He slapped his knee in excitement. "It's in your blood. Annie Block of acting stock!"

Charlotte rolled her eyes at Annie. Her dad could be so corny. But Annie didn't see. A determined look had come over her face. "I'm going to do it," she said. "I'm going to start tonight. I'll even be Carlotta in my sleep!"

"Good for you, Annie!" Mr. Cheetham stood up. "Concentration, that's all it will take. Talent you already have."

"Don't wait in the morning," Annie said to

Charlotte at the door. "I'd better walk alone. Concentrate."

Charlotte would believe *that* when she saw it! Annie hated walking to school alone, even on normal days. How could she do it on the scariest day of her life?

"Good night, Annie," Mr. Cheetham said. "And good luck."

"Luck?" Annie lifted her chin. "Who needs that? I have magic, darlings. If Tina wins—zap, she's a frog!"

13

The next morning, Annie wasn't on the corner. She was nowhere in sight. Had she really gone all the way to school being Carlotta? Or had she chickened out? Charlotte bet anything she'd chickened out. Poor Annie. Charlotte hurried on to school. And poor *her*. Tina would gloat for the rest of her life.

But Annie was in her seat! Charlotte felt goose bumps rush along her arms. She couldn't believe Annie would really have the nerve to do it. She tried to catch her eye, but Annie wouldn't look up.

All morning, Annie stared into space. Charlotte hoped that behind her blank look she was busy being Carlotta. Behind the blank look *could* be a blank brain—Annie trying to disappear.

At lunch, Annie wouldn't say a word.

"Just tell me," Charlotte whispered. "Are you going to do it, or not?"

Annie didn't reply. It was like she wasn't even there.

"My parents are getting divorced," Charlotte said. No answer. "And we're moving to Brazil." Annie didn't blink. "Pippi died," Charlotte added. "Sam, too." Okay, that was it! Annie could talk for one little minute, concentration or not. "Cut it out!" Charlotte ordered. "Just tell me. Are you going to do it, or not?"

Annie suddenly turned alert eyes in Charlotte's direction. She seemed mildly surprised to see her sitting there. She smiled.

"Ever eat this magic-meat?" she asked, opening her sandwich and letting bologna plop out of the bread.

Charlotte frowned. What did that mean?

Annie rolled the bologna into a log and bit it. "Magic-meat," she repeated in a sing-songy voice. "Made from mustard and old crow's feet. The less you need it, the more you eat." She chuckled and stuffed the whole piece into her mouth.

Charlotte's own mouth fell open. So did those of Tina and Jenny, who were staring from across the table. Charlotte closed her mouth. She

89

smiled. Cute little Carlotta couldn't have said it better.

"Now, let's see." Mrs. Sanchez scanned the sign-up sheet, then looked up. "Why don't we do Scene One first. It has Carlotta and both little witches."

Charlotte began to sweat. A whole river ran down her back.

Mrs. Sanchez looked a little nervous too. She was fidgeting with the edges of the script. "We'll need one of our Carlottas,"she murmured. She cleared her throat. "And a Little Witch One and a Little Witch Two. Jenny, you come try out for Little Witch One. Laura, Little Witch Two."

The girls hurried eagerly to the front of the class, clutching their scripts.

The teacher looked from Tina to Annie and back to Tina. "Annie," she decided. "You'll be first. Tina will go tomorrow."

Tina shrugged. She draped her arm across the back of her chair, preparing herself to be bored to death.

Annie walked to the front of the class.

"You've forgotten your script, dear," Mrs. Sanchez said. She gestured her back. "Hurry and get it."

Annie went back to her desk and returned with the script. She smiled pleasantly at Mrs. Sanchez.

"All right, let's begin." Mrs. Sanchez moved away. "Act One, Scene One. Witch Headquarters."

The first line was Annie's. Everyone stared at her, waiting. Charlotte's heart was pounding so hard she thought it might knock her out of her seat. Annie didn't speak. What was she waiting for?

Annie picked up her script. She ripped off the first page and carefully folded it up. She ripped off page two. No one—not even the teacher—said a word. They were all too surprised. Annie kept ripping.

Finally, Annie looked up. She held one of the folded pages over her head. It had been creased into the shape of a paper airplane.

" 'Life is so boring,' " she said loudly, with a sigh. It was the first line of the play. She sailed the airplane into space. " 'Are you two going to sit there all day like dumb little witches and just study?' " She launched another plane. This one crashed into the blackboard behind the teacher's head.

Little Witch One was supposed to reply, but Jenny looked stunned. Mrs. Sanchez reached out and gave her a nudge. "Oh," she said. " 'Yes. I plan to learn the most chants of any witch on earth. I want to be president one day.' " An airplane whizzed by her ear.

Annie rolled her eyes. " 'Darlings,' " she said.
" 'No one gets to be president by studying. We
all know that. It takes flair. Flair is the most important thing there is. Look at me. *I* never
study.' "

Little Witch One hastily scanned her script.
" 'Yes,' " she said. " 'Look at you. Just wasting
time day and night. You'll be sorry one day. Someday there'll be great danger in the land and only
one of us good little witches can help. You won't
be able to, because you won't know the chants.' "

" 'Yeah,' " said Laura, Little Witch Two.
" '*We'll* be the heroes.' "

Annie fired off another plane. It somersaulted crazily across the room and sailed to the floor. No one even ducked. They were all too busy watching Annie to care.

" 'My darlings,' " Annie said slowly, giving her hair a shake and then patting it carefully back into place. " 'When there is danger in the land, you come right here to Carlotta. We'll see who the hero is.' " She placed her hands on her hips and turned her back to them all. Proudly, she marched back to her seat, glancing over her shoulder only once with a haughty look.

No one said a word. Even Charlotte was speechless. In her wildest imagination she hadn't hoped for *that*.

"Wow," George said finally.

Wow.

The funny thing was, Annie went right back to being herself afterward. When people crowded around her desk to congratulate her, she just blushed and looked like plain old Annie.

Suddenly, there was Tina. "That was dumb!" she announced. "Carlotta isn't six years old. She wouldn't throw paper airplanes. The script doesn't say to, either."

Everyone looked at Annie.

Annie's eyes seemed to glaze over. Then they cleared. She looked Tina right in the face. "So what?" she said. "When you have flair, who needs a script?"

"I can't believe you did that," Charlotte said on the way home. She meant both things—the audition and talking back to Tina. "You changed into another person."

Annie nodded. "I know. It's weird, huh? I just tried what your dad said. I thought and thought and thought about being Carlotta. I tried to *feel* like her. And then—I don't know. I just *was*. And I forgot everything else."

Charlotte didn't think she could do that even if she thought and thought. She'd always be wondering what people in the audience were saying or doing. Annie hadn't even looked to see.

"I guess it's like when you used to lie," Annie said thoughtfully. "You know? You always believed your lies when you were telling them. That's how I felt today."

Yes, but Charlotte hadn't been able to control her lies. She couldn't just turn them on and off and plan how to use them. They'd popped into her head and out her mouth all by themselves. What Annie did was different. Much different. She *worked* at being Carlotta and then did it. She was probably even more of a genius at acting than Charlotte was at writing.

Charlotte studied her friend from the corner of her eye as they walked. For one second she was jealous. But only for a second. She'd wanted Annie to be a star and now she was. How could she ever be jealous of that?

"How'd she do?" her father asked the minute she walked in the door.

"She did great." Charlotte dropped her books onto the kitchen table and pretended to search through them. Something was wrong with her voice—it wasn't excited, like it should be. She hoped her father didn't notice.

He didn't. "Honestly? She actually pulled it off? She got up there and *acted*?" He looked like he'd won the lottery and two art awards all at once.

Charlotte nodded. "They loved her, too."

Her father slapped his fist into his hand. "I knew it! I knew she could do it! Tell me everything. All about it."

So Charlotte described the paper airplanes and how Annie had sung the chants in the perfect sing-songy way and how she'd even talked back to Tina. She was amazed all over again, remembering. It really had been great.

Her father looked dazed. "Wow," he said. He rumpled Charlotte's hair the way he did when he was pleased, but he didn't seem to know he did it. And it was Annie he was pleased with, not her.

Charlotte watched him wander off toward his studio, happily shaking his head. He hadn't asked one thing about her day. Didn't he want to know what his daughter the director thought about auditions?

At that moment Pippi rushed through the kitchen and down the stairs to the cat door that led to the yard. She was getting so fat the door slowed her down. It didn't slow her down enough for her to notice Charlotte, though. She wasn't *looking* for Charlotte, that was why. No one was.

14

Tina stomped her feet and flung out her arms. " 'Life is so boring,' " she yelled. " 'Are you two going to sit there all day like dumb little witches and just study?' " She bent across Sarah, who was Little Witch One, and snarled. Sarah looked so alarmed she forgot to reply. Tina kicked at the leg of her desk.

"For goodness' sakes, Tina," Mrs. Sanchez murmured.

" 'Yes,' " Sarah said meekly, leaning away. " 'I plan to learn the most chants of any witch on earth. I want to be president one day.' "

Tina ripped the first page off Sarah's script and wadded it into a ball. She flung it at Sarah's head.

" 'That's not how you get to be president, stupid,' " she said. " 'It takes flair!' "

"Tina!" Mrs. Sanchez looked shocked. "That's

quite enough. I don't think the script calls for the word 'stupid.' Or for violence."

Tina turned red. "The script didn't call for paper airplanes, did it? This is what *I* think Carlotta would do."

They stared at each other. "All right," Mrs. Sanchez said finally. "Go on."

Tina went on. She stomped around the stage and ranted and raved for the whole first scene. Sarah and Jenny, who was Little Witch Two, began to giggle whenever she spoke. It *was* pretty funny. Mrs. Sanchez turned her back and pressed her fingertips to her forehead. Soon everyone in the class was snickering, even Charlotte, who was supposed to be a judge. She couldn't help it.

Suddenly Tina stopped. She looked around the room. Everyone fell silent, but Tina's fierce look began to waver. To their amazement, she burst into tears and rushed from the room. No one said a word. They couldn't believe it. Tina *crying*?

"All right, girls," Mrs. Sanchez said quietly to Jenny and Sarah. "Take your seats. All of you please read for a while." She hurried from the room.

When she returned, Tina wasn't with her. Wherever she was, she stayed there all day.

*　*　*

"Did you believe that?" Charlotte said on the way home. "I mean Tina *cried*." Charlotte actually felt sorry for her. She couldn't believe *that*, either.

"I couldn't believe how bad she was," Annie said cheerfully. "She really can't act, just like Mrs. Sanchez said. She's only noise."

Charlotte was shocked. Tina hadn't come back all day. What if she'd run away? Or jumped off a bridge? It was a rotten thing to say right now. And *Annie Block* had said it!

Hey, what was going on? Someone had locked Pippi in Charlotte's bedroom. Charlotte hurried angrily down the hall to Ruth's room. Ruth was supposed to keep *her* pet locked up, not Charlotte's. That was the deal.

Ruth's door was closed too. Pippi, who'd followed at her heels, began to claw and meow.

"Don't open it!" Ruth screeched. "And lock up the cat! Sam's out."

Sam was out? Charlotte rushed Pippi back to the bedroom and locked her inside. It was absolutely against the rules for Sam to be out in Ruth's room. He wasn't mature enough yet. Charlotte hurried back to see what was going on.

"Pippi's locked up," she called. "Let me in."

The door opened a crack. Marie peeked out. "Hurry," she whispered, gesturing wildly for her to come in. Charlotte slid through the crack and slammed the door behind her. Sam was nowhere in sight.

"He's up there," Ruth said tearfully. Sam sat calmly on the curtain rod over her window. "And he won't come down. If I had him stick trained, he'd step off onto a stick."

Charlotte nodded as if she'd known that all along.

"He almost flew into the window." Ruth's voice shook. She didn't take her eyes off the bird. "He could have had a concussion. He could have died!"

"Mom told you that," Marie said. "She told you that very thing would happen if you let him out before he was ready."

"I didn't let him out!" Ruth said angrily.

"Well, then how'd he get up there?" Charlotte asked.

Ruth didn't reply. She stared up at Sam with a quivering chin.

"She was cleaning his water dish," Marie whispered. "And decided to give him a kiss." She rolled her eyes at Charlotte and Ruth turned red. Actually, Charlotte sympathized. It was something she might do.

Outside, a car door slammed.

"You're going to get it," Marie said.

Charlotte wondered suddenly why people

100

spent so much time being mean. It made her tired just thinking of all the meanness there was around.

In a flash, Sam swooped from the curtain rod to his cage. He poised for a moment on the rim of the door and then flew inside to his perch. Ruth rushed forward to close the door. Downstairs, Mrs. Cheetham called hello.

"Well," Ruth said sheepishly. "It's nice she won't have to know." She looked imploringly at her sisters.

Charlotte nodded. *She* wasn't going to tell. Marie better not either.

Walking down the hall to her room, she thought of how weird the last two days had been. She'd felt sorry for Tina. She'd felt sorry for Ruth.

And for a few minutes she hadn't liked her own father and her best friend at all.

Tina came to school the next day looking the same as ever. Even grumpier, in fact. She bumped against Annie's desk, and Annie's books slid to the floor.

"Cut it out, Tina," Laura said, bending to pick them up. Annie gave her a grateful smile.

Charlotte glared at them. Laura was only being nice because she thought Annie was going to be the star. It was exactly what had happened to Charlotte last year when she wrote her book. Annie had been the first to see what two-faced rats they were. Now she was beaming at Laura like she was the kindest kid on earth.

"Charlotte?" Mrs. Sanchez waved her to the front of the class. On her way, Charlotte had the urge to bump Laura's desk. There was a big stack of books that would slide right off. She didn't do it. Annie would just help her pick them up.

Mrs. Sanchez wanted to discuss auditions. She assigned the class a reading-aloud project and led Charlotte to the storage room across the hall. She left both doors open so she could spy.

They sat in two kindergarten chairs. "Isn't Annie going to be wonderful?" Mrs. Sanchez said happily, opening the notebook in her lap. "You were right."

Charlotte frowned. It seemed to her that they ought to at least discuss auditions and not just *say* Annie was going to get the part. But looking at Mrs. Sanchez's face, she knew the truth— Annie would have gotten the lead no matter what, as long as she could talk. Mrs. Sanchez didn't want Tina to have it. Deep down inside Charlotte had felt that way too, but she'd tried to be fair. Shouldn't a teacher try too?

Mrs. Sanchez caught sight of Charlotte's face. She closed her notebook. "You know," she said seriously, "I feel sorry for Tina. Very sorry. This part was important to her and losing it will be a very big blow."

Charlotte nodded. She felt sorry for Tina too. On the other hand, Tina *was* a rat. She caused Charlotte to have very big blows every day. Also, she couldn't act. Charlotte sighed. Being fair sure was confusing.

Mrs. Sanchez sighed along with her. "It's just that I think Tina needs to learn a few things before it's too late," she said softly. "That she isn't always going to get her way in life, for one."

Charlotte considered it. "She never needed to know that before," she said. "It was never true."

Mrs. Sanchez laughed loudly. Across the hall, whoever was reading stopped.

15

So Annie was Carlotta and Peter was Morgan. Jenny and Laura were Little Witch One and Little Witch Two. Robert and George and Michael were innocent trick-or-treaters. Sarah was Homeowner Number One. Frank was Homeowner Number Two. Jeffrey was Morgan's assistant. Everyone else worked props.

No one, Mrs. Sanchez pointed out, was Great Grumble Witch. "How about it?" she asked cheerfully of the prop workers. "Let's have a volunteer. It's a part you can really have fun with."

Tina snorted.

"How about you, Tina?" the teacher said. There was a note of challenge in her voice.

Tina folded her arms. "You said I couldn't,"

she pointed out smugly. "You said if I didn't get the part I tried out for, I'd just work props."

Mrs. Sanchez blushed. "I suppose I did. But I've changed my mind."

Tina shrugged. "Tough."

Everyone stared. No one—not even Tina—could talk to a teacher like that!

Mrs. Sanchez very calmly opened her notebook and made a few notes. "Now," she said. "I'd like to start rehearsals soon. And costumes, of course. And scenery. Most of it will be done during class time, but I'd like to meet with you one by one after school to discuss what you'll wear. Except for Tina. I think that as Great Grumble Witch, you can just be creative. Anything outrageous will do."

Everyone looked at Tina. Now *she* turned red. She didn't say anything though. Somehow, the teacher had won.

Charlotte sat in the back row and watched. They were rehearsing on the stage. There were a million things they were doing wrong, too. If anyone had ever read her Director's Book, they'd know. Right on page one she'd written, "Never allow actors to step out of character during scenes." Well, that's what kids were doing. Especially Peter. When he didn't have lines to say, he shot rubber bands at George. And Tina didn't grunt unless the teacher made her. She just sat on the stage like a lump. Great Grumble Witch was supposed to make the audience laugh.

Also, kids weren't speaking clearly at all. Charlotte flipped to the part in her notebook about dentalizing. If you placed your tongue against the back of your teeth and *then* talked, "th" words came out clearer. "This," she whispered, with the emphasis on the *th*. It was a good thing to practice every day.

Mrs. Sanchez wasn't having kids do any of these things. Charlotte could tell she'd never read even one of Mrs. Arnold's books on acting. And she'd also never asked for Charlotte's help. Every day she had rehearsals all planned before they even got to school, and every day rehearsals were just the same. Peter shot rubber bands. Tina didn't grunt. The play sounded dumb the way they did it. Charlotte was going to hate her own play!

"All right, everybody!" Mrs. Sanchez clapped her hands. "I think we're losing our concentration."

Losing it? Ten minutes ago Tina had slid to the floor when the teacher wasn't looking. She still sat there. And every time the teacher turned her back, Peter made faces at George. Now Tina stuck

106

her foot out as Peter rushed by and he tripped. Everyone laughed.

"Stop it," Mrs. Sanchez said angrily. "In case you don't know it, this play is only two weeks away. You'll be here onstage in front of everyone in school *and their parents*. Do you understand?"

This silenced them. Tina even slid back up to her seat.

"Charlotte?" Mrs. Sanchez turned suddenly to the back of the auditorium. "What do you think? You must have some suggestions."

Charlotte was startled. Of course she had suggestions! It was her *job* to have suggestions, but she'd given up expecting anyone to ask about them.

"Charlotte?" Mrs. Sanchez squinted in her direction. "Aren't you there? I *know* you have something to say."

Everyone laughed. Okay then, she *did* have something to say! Charlotte stood up and marched to the foot of the stage, clutching her Director's Book.

"Yes," she said. "I do. You're all doing everything wrong. For one thing, Peter shouldn't be chewing gum. Or shooting rubber bands." Charlotte stopped. She sounded obnoxious, even to herself, but she knew she couldn't stop. A whole flood of sentences had built up inside her head and every one of them was going to come out.

Peter was so surprised he stopped chewing. "And nobody pays attention between speeches," Charlotte went on. "If you don't have a line to say, you're still supposed to listen and be who you are. When Peter isn't Morgan, he just fools around. And Tina sits there like a lump. She's supposed to be grunting at all the right times." Tina and Peter both scowled.

"It's a well-taken point, Charlotte," Mrs. Sanchez said approvingly. "When you act, you *act*. That means being your character for the duration of the play. What else do you suggest?"

"People need to speak more clearly. I think you should practice dentalizing for a while."

Mrs. Sanchez looked surprised. Onstage, Tina gave a grunt.

"I'm not certain what you mean, Charlotte," Mrs. Sanchez said uneasily.

Charlotte clenched her teeth and placed her tongue against them. "It's talking like *th*is," she said carefully. "*Their. Thing. Th*istle."

Boos and hisses suddenly arose from the stage. A rubber band pelted Charlotte's ear. "Thistle!" Peter shrieked uproariously. Everyone joined in. A chorus of *thistle*s and hoots filled the air. Tina slid again from her chair. "Thistle," she said as she thumped.

"Stop it!" Mrs. Sanchez turned on the class. "Charlotte is absolutely right. She's telling you exactly what you need to hear. She means enunciate. You all need to enunciate."

"I need to crunch-iate, myself," Peter said under his breath. "Crunch-iate Charlotte Cheetham."

Mrs. Sanchez marched up onto the stage. Charlotte had never seen her look so mad. Even Peter looked alarmed.

The teacher bent close to him, hands on her hips. "Would you like to repeat that, Peter?" she asked quietly. Her face was only inches away from his.

Peter stepped back. He opened his eyes in a wide, innocent look. "Repeat what?" he asked with a croak.

Mrs. Sanchez stepped forward. "I think, Peter," she persisted, "that we'd all like to hear you dentalize an apology to Charlotte. Right now." She folded her arms.

Peter was backed against the wall. He peered around the teacher and gave Charlotte the kind of phony smile that announced he would kill her at some future date. "I'm very sorry, Charlotte," he said carefully, enunciating each word. "I a-pol-o-gize."

"I thought your ideas were great," Annie said on the way home. "The play was much better after you said all that."

109

Charlotte didn't reply. Sure it had been better. Mrs. Sanchez had been so mad she'd have murdered them if it hadn't been. Charlotte couldn't believe what a fool she'd made of herself. She'd acted exactly like Miss Brown, her teacher from last year, telling everybody what to do in a bossy voice. Mrs. Sanchez had been nice about it, pretending Charlotte had done a perfectly normal thing, but Charlotte knew the truth. She hadn't done one perfectly normal thing in her whole life and she probably never would.

16

"How's the play coming?" her father asked at dinner.

"Okay. Fine. Great." Charlotte didn't want to talk about the play, but saying so would make the opposite happen.

"Did you tell Mrs. Sanchez about my offer to make props?" He wanted to make bushes out of some green wire mesh he'd found at the university and picket fences out of some old gates in the garage. Sometimes he was just like a kid.

"Yes. I told her. She said 'marvelous' and 'why don't you come to rehearsal sometime?' " Charlotte choked on the words as soon as she said them. A stage full of laughing, booing, hissing, hysterical people flashed before her eyes. Her father couldn't come to rehearsal! Charlotte would die if he did!

Suddenly from the backyard came the sound of barking and a loud cat shriek. Charlotte shot up in alarm. Pippi! She rushed for the door, but before she could get there, Pippi came barreling through the little opening down below. She didn't pause for as much as a wiggle, and the plastic frame of the door came with her, circling her middle like a hula skirt. She slunk into the room, ears flat, body low, clearly unharmed but terrified by both the creature in the yard and the one that now clutched her chubby middle.

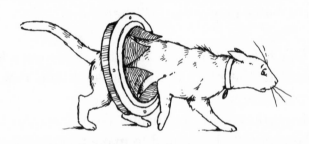

Everyone, except Charlotte, began to laugh. Ruth and Marie laughed so hard they fell off their chairs, scaring poor Pippi even more. How could they be so mean? All of them? Even Charlotte's mother!

Charlotte swept Pippi off her feet and carried her squirming, plastic and all, up the stairs to her room. Pippi had been smart to hurry when a huge dog was after her! Was it her fault Mr. Cheetham had put on a flimsy door? Why didn't everyone laugh at *him*?

Charlotte dropped the cat onto her bed and gently pulled the frame loose. "Don't let those jerks bother you," she said, pressing her cheek against Pippi's fur. What had happened to Pippi was exactly what had happened to her at school. Kids had laughed at Charlotte, when it was Peter and Tina who were being dumb. Sure, she'd been bossy, but she'd been *right*. Every single thing she'd said was true, and if they'd listen to her, the play would be great. She was *supposed* to tell them what to do. That's what directors did.

From now on she was going to direct. If she had to be bossy all the time, she would.

Peter glared at Charlotte from the stage. "You're full of it, Charlotte," he said. Mrs. Sanchez had stepped out of the auditorium to find some missing props. Charlotte was in charge.

Charlotte glared back. "I am not! You're supposed to look nervous in this scene, not make faces at the prop workers!"

Peter stuck out his tongue and crossed his eyes. Behind him, Tina gave a grunt. She was grunting at all the wrong times and making everyone laugh. It was spoiling the whole thing.

"Stop it, Tina!" Charlotte said angrily. Tina grunted again, this time to the tune of "Old MacDonald Had a Farm." Charlotte flung her Director's Book onto the floor. They didn't care!

This play wasn't serious to them at all. And she was sick of trying to make them care.

"Let's start over," Annie said calmly. Surprisingly, everyone listened. They moved back into their places.

Charlotte picked up her book and carried it to a seat in the front row. Corners of two of the pages had ripped. She felt tears rise into her eyes as she smoothed them out. Don't cry, she ordered herself. Directors never cry. But why did everyone listen to Annie and not to her? Lately every time Annie had an idea they all said, "Great," no matter how weird it was, but not one person had liked Charlotte's idea of having the crystal ball turn into a pumpkin at midnight, and *that* was a great idea.

"What do *you* think, Charlotte?" Annie called down from the stage.

Charlotte looked up. They were staring at her. It figured! The one time she wasn't listening, they asked for directorly advice.

She cleared her throat and quickly turned a page. "What was the question?" she asked, sounding busy.

"Peter thinks he should *pull* the trick-or-treaters into the tent, but I think they should just *go*."

Charlotte frowned. For one second she wished Annie were wrong, but she wasn't, of course.

"He wouldn't have to pull," she agreed. "His tricks make them *want* to go in."

"But it's supposed to be scary!" Peter batted at the tent. "It's not scary if they just walk in."

"The audience knows you're going to kill them, Peter," Charlotte said. "That's pretty scary." Honestly! Peter still didn't understand his own part. He just wanted to do whatever got him attention.

"Well, maybe he could say something," Annie said thoughtfully. "Like 'Gotcha!' or 'Tricked again!' I mean after they're inside."

Jenny nodded. "Or he could rub his hands together and cackle. 'Heh, heh, heh.' Something like that."

Annie shrugged. "Okay. He can do that." This time no one asked Charlotte's opinion. Annie the Great had spoken.

The scene went perfectly. There wasn't one thing for Charlotte to correct. No one stepped out of role. No one mumbled or said lines at the wrong time. It was good. It was great. Charlotte didn't feel the least bit glad.

"Rehearsal was perfect," Annie said on the way home. She gave a little skip of excitement. "After you yelled, everyone got serious. It was like a real play!"

115

It was true. But not because Charlotte had yelled. Because Annie had calmed them down.

"And I made some more scenery!" Annie glowed. "Did you see it? I drew a black cat on a picket fence and a full moon in the sky. I think it's pretty good."

Charlotte had seen it. It was great.

Annie didn't seem to notice that Charlotte wasn't talking. She was too busy talking herself.

"Maybe I can come see Pippi today," she said next. It was more of a statement than a question.

Charlotte shook her head. "I have work to do." The last thing she needed was to see Pippi rubbing and purring all over Annie. Besides, her father might be home. He'd want to hear every detail about rehearsal and his "star." His "star" had been great, but that was partly because she had a great play to be a star in. People had stopped mentioning that.

Annie nodded, accepting it. She didn't even look sad at the news.

17

"I'm calling my report 'The Bird that Meows,' "
Ruth announced at dinner, as if it were a major
world event.

"Sounds fine," Mr. Cheetham said. Charlotte
could tell he wasn't really interested. He was only
being nice.

"Mr. Bergen says if I write it up like a newspaper article with pictures and all, he'll submit it
to the paper. Sam might be in the news!"

Charlotte dropped her fork. That was disgusting! *Pippi* was the reason Sam meowed. Sam was
only copying. It didn't take brains for that. It took
brains to figure out when to go in and out a cat
door when there was a world full of danger outside. It took brains to know there was a bird in
Ruth's room when her door was shut and the
bird was quiet!

"So Sam has become a media event," Mr. Cheetham said cheerfully, as if someone from the paper had already stopped by.

"I believe Mr. Bergen said *might*," Charlotte said loudly. "Sam *might* be in the news. If nothing else happens in the world that day."

Ruth flung a dinner roll across the table and ended the discussion.

Mrs. Sanchez looked worriedly up at the stage. Every time Carlotta had tried to come crashing through, the green wire bushes had fallen and rolled. So now she had arranged them in a row and tied them with string. Carlotta was supposed to get hung up in the bushes, not drag them across the stage. "What do you think, Charlotte?" she asked. "Does the string show too much?"

Charlotte shook her head. "Not really." But now Carlotta would probably trip on the string. She didn't mention this to Mrs. Sanchez, who was already a wreck. Mr. Cheetham was coming to watch the rehearsal today. It was the first time another grown-up would see the play.

The rehearsal went well. Tina accidentally fell off her chair, but somehow it was okay. It was the sort of thing Great Grumble Witch might do. And once, when Peter messed up his lines, he started to giggle, but when no one giggled back, he stopped. They were serious, like real actors in a real play.

When it was over, Mr. Cheetham looked a little dazed. "Wow," he said softly. Mrs. Sanchez had tears in her eyes. Happy tears. Charlotte's old excitement had returned. Her heart fluttered so wildly she could hardly see or hear. She'd watched her father watch the play and he'd loved it! So had Mrs. Sanchez. So had *Charlotte.*

Her father ran his hand through his hair and gave his head a little shake as if to bring himself back to earth. "Incredible," he said. "Absolutely incredible." But he wasn't looking at Charlotte. He was staring at the stage. Charlotte suddenly saw—it was Annie he was looking at! And Annie he was talking about?

"She *was* incredible, wasn't she?" Charlotte asked. It was a trick question. If her father said, "Who?" then he'd been talking about the play. If he said, "Yes"—

He finally looked at Charlotte. "Oh yes," he said quietly, his eyes bright. "She certainly was."

After school, Annie and Charlotte and her dad stayed to talk over the scenery and costumes and the programs Mrs. Sanchez had designed on the high school's computer.

"Can you believe it?" Mr. Cheetham said elatedly as he drove them home. "Annie Block a star!"

Annie giggled. She was seated beside him in the front.

In the backseat, Charlotte stared gloomily out the window and didn't talk. Her father had just promised to paint Annie a glittery star for her bedroom door. He wasn't painting Charlotte one.

" 'Bye, Charlotte," Annie said when they dropped her off. " 'Bye, coach!" She giggled again and waved happily from the sidewalk.

Mr. Cheetham smiled and waved back. "Good-

bye, 'darling,' " he called. "Get yourself a good night's sleep. You have to keep up your energy for the show!"

Charlotte fumed. She bet he wouldn't bother

to say that to *her* tonight. Directors weren't important enough to need sleep.

Ruth and Marie were in the kitchen loading film into the Polaroid camera.

Ruth smiled. "Too bad we didn't have this when Pippi was modeling her cat door," she said.

Charlotte stomped right by, but they followed her up the stairs.

"I have to take pictures of Sam," Ruth said loudly. "For my report."

Charlotte turned into her room, and they went on down the hall. How could she ever have felt sympathy for Ruth? How could she ever have felt sympathy for anyone in the world? Remember how she'd felt sorry for Annie when she couldn't act? Now look what had happened. Annie had practically stolen her dad. Tears ran down Charlotte's cheeks, but she wiped them away. Ruth was coming.

"You have the TV tray?" she asked, barging in.

It so happened Charlotte did. She'd put it next to her desk when she was making her Director's Book so she could spread things out. She shrugged. She wasn't going to make anything easy for Ruth.

Ruth spotted it for herself. She crossed the room and dumped the things on it onto the floor.

"How do you know I don't need that?" Charlotte asked furiously. She followed Ruth down the hall. "I might need it right now!"

Ruth set the tray in front of the window. "*I* need it now," she said. "I want Sam in front of the window so I don't have to use a flash. I don't want to scare my poor baby," she said as she and Marie carefully moved the cage. She was talking baby talk to a bird!

The cage barely fit on the tray, but Ruth jiggled it into place.

"Okay, Sammie," she said as she held the camera to her face. "Smile!"

As if a bird could smile! But Sam did cock his head in a funny little way that made it look like he was posing. Ruth took every picture in the pack, and they all came out great.

"Let's take them downstairs and spread them out," she said eagerly to Marie. "I want the best one for the cover. And that will probably be the one that goes in the paper, too." She flashed a superior smile at Charlotte as they left.

Charlotte stared at Sam. He cocked his head. The afternoon light coming in the window made the two orange setting suns on his cheeks especially bright. Charlotte felt all the anger melt right out of her. He was so little and sweet. She wished everyone in the world were as sweet as this bird.

Sam hopped onto his swing and turned around. With his back to her, he began to swing. It seemed to Charlotte that he was enjoying the sun and the window and the change of scenery. It was so cute she began to ache. He began to swing fast. Faster and faster, until even the TV tray trembled a bit. Once or twice he paused to look back. Charlotte suddenly understood. He was showing off! He wanted to make sure she was watching to see how high he got. She couldn't believe it. Sam was just like Ruth! Not to mention a few other stars in the world.

"I hope you swing yourself into outer space," Charlotte whispered. "Dumb thing." But Sam didn't seem to hear. He just kept going, higher and higher, having himself a wonderful time. Showing off.

18

and with final-look for it in the day with.
have from the made of the two panic life.
two life-will has the two with the two.
to a with it. He began be-tried it is tried.
two-will in the two of-because-with of it.
my truth of the life for in the two. Should.
half two to their with it to the little.
to of-to said the two-will a-with the two.
all it-as-will-it as a-same with the little. Still.
couldn't-it make some say the little. Still.
to mention a few others alike in the world.

"Oof!" Annie had rushed too quickly through the bushes and tripped on the string. She tumbled to the center of the stage, dragging a jumble of green wire mesh behind her.

"Oh, goodness," Mrs. Sanchez said, rushing to her aid. "Are you all right?"

Annie shook herself loose and stood up. She brushed at her jeans. "I think so," she said breathlessly.

Jenny crossed her arms on her chest. "I thought you'd broken your ankle," she exclaimed. "And the play's next week!"

"Oh, heavens!" Mrs. Sanchez looked ill. "Don't say that!"

"What would we do if somebody got sick or hurt?" Laura asked thoughtfully. "Nobody else knows our parts."

"Charlotte does." Jenny looked at her. "She knows every single line."

Mrs. Sanchez breathed a visible sigh of relief. "This is true. But since there's only one Charlotte and lots of you, please don't anyone get hurt!" She laughed.

Charlotte tried to laugh too, but something strange was going on in her stomach. She had a really sharp pain. She'd watched Annie lying on the stage and thought that very thought: If Annie were hurt, *she* would get the lead. Charlotte tried to pretend she hadn't thought it, but she had. She had.

Ruth charged through the living room, her face streaked with tears. She brushed past Charlotte without seeing her. "Dad!" she shrieked. "Dad!"

Mr. Cheetham ran from his studio.

"It's Sam!" Ruth clutched at his arm and rushed him toward the stairs. Charlotte followed. At the top of the steps, Marie was jiggling anxiously, her hands clamped across her mouth.

In Ruth's room, Sam's cage lay on the floor. Inside the cage lay Sam. Not moving.

"He's dead," Ruth shrieked hysterically.

Mr. Cheetham bent over the cage. The water dish and bell and feeder had all come loose. Even the swing was broken. Everything in the cage lay in a jumble about Sam's body. "Maybe not," he whispered, as if even the sound of his voice might cause a landslide. "Maybe he's only stunned."

"Then get him out!" Ruth cried.

Mr. Cheetham studied the cage. He slowly shook his head. "The cage landed on its door," he said quietly. "If I pick it up, he might get hurt."

"But he already *is* hurt!" Marie said. She was still jiggling.

Mr. Cheetham stood up and looked around. "How did this happen?" he asked. He saw the TV tray on its side on the floor. "You didn't have him on that flimsy thing?"

Ruth wailed and flung herself onto the bed.

"He liked it there," Charlotte said weakly. "In the sun."

Mr. Cheetham frowned, but he didn't comment. He looked back down at the cage. Charlotte looked too. She knew the truth: Sam was dead.

Quietly, she left the room. She couldn't stand the sight of the little bird lying there in his cage, his toys all around him like that. It was the saddest thing she'd ever seen. She remembered how happy he'd looked, rocking wildly back and forth. So what if he'd been showing off? He was special. He had a right to show off. Charlotte had just been jealous because he was Ruth's. "Rock yourself into outer space," she'd told him, and that was what he'd done. It was all her fault!

"I'm sorry, Sam," she whispered, lying face down on her bed. She couldn't even cry. She felt too shocked and ashamed and empty to cry. She hoped that Sam would know: She cared as much as anyone. As much as Ruth. Even more, because she was the reason he'd died.

The next morning was Saturday. They held a funeral for Sam in the backyard. Mrs. Cheetham laid him in a shoe box with his broken swing and his toys, and they buried the box in a deep hole beside the garage. If you looked up, you could see Ruth's window where his cage had sat. No one did.

"Maybe Ruth can get another bird," Marie said as they all walked slowly toward the house.

"Another bird won't be Sam!" Ruth's chin quivered.

Charlotte agreed. In the kitchen she stared at Pippi. She'd never want another cat if something happened to Pippi. Charlotte didn't pet her. It didn't seem fair that she still had her cat when Sam was dead.

"I'm not going to any dumb Halloween party, either!" Ruth shouted. In the corner lay her shredded costume, the victim of an earlier rage.

127

She'd been planning on being a bird. Now the giant feathers were bent and twisted every which way. Ruth scooped up the costume and flung it across the room. Pippi pounced and rolled as it landed. She ran off with one of the feathers between her teeth.

It was the final straw. Ruth fell into a chair at the table and sobbed. Charlotte didn't blame her one bit.

"After school, you want to gather leaves?" Annie asked Monday morning.

Charlotte shook her head. They *should* gather leaves. They needed boxfuls to dump around onstage. She just didn't want to do it. She didn't want to do anything.

"Are you mad at me lately or something?" Annie asked quietly.

Charlotte's eyes watered. She blinked them, hard. How could Annie even care? Charlotte was a disgusting person who killed birds and wished her best friend bad luck and that friend still wanted her to like her.

"Are you, Charlotte?" Annie pursued. "You never talk. And every day you act like you're mad, even though the play's really good."

Charlotte stopped walking. She stared at her feet. What could she say—I *was* mad? I wished you were hurt and I wished you couldn't act and

I wished my dad didn't like you, even though you're my best friend and the nicest person I ever met? Charlotte had to say something. She could feel Annie staring.

"Sam died." Charlotte's chin quivered. It was true and it was sad, but it was such a tiny piece of the real truth that it felt like a lie. Saying it only made things worse.

Annie gasped. "Oh, Charlotte! That's awful!"

Charlotte nodded. It was awful. And she knew, suddenly, that she couldn't go to school with such awfulness rumbling around inside her. She felt stuffed to the eyeballs with awfulness, like she might explode. "I think I'm sick," she said to Annie. "I *know* I'm sick. I might throw up. Tell Mrs. Sanchez." She backed away.

Annie stared after her in concern. Charlotte really did feel sick. She really was going to throw up. At the corner she turned and ran.

"You don't have a fever," her mother said thoughtfully, running her hand across Charlotte's forehead. "You don't look sick."

"It's my stomach," Charlotte clutched at it. It hurt a lot. Maybe her appendix was about to burst. That had happened to her cousin in Texas last year. They had had to operate to save her life.

Her mother looked dismayed. "I can't stay

home, Charlotte. I'm at a crucial point at the lab. And Dad's at the university until one."

Charlotte nodded. "That's all right." She didn't want anyone to help. She didn't want anyone to take care of her, or even feed her, or even save her life if her appendix burst. No one had saved Sam's.

At four o'clock, her father peered into her room. "Annie's downstairs," he said.

Charlotte pulled the covers over her head. Her father had stuck his head in every fifteen minutes since one o'clock and tried to make her talk. This might be another trick or it might not. It didn't matter. Charlotte didn't want to see anyone, Annie included.

At dinnertime, her mother brought her broth and ran her hand across her forehead for the two-hundredth time. Charlotte pulled away. She peered at the soup, and her stomach gurgled.

"I can't eat," she said, and meant it.

19

Charlotte stayed home the next day, too. She pictured Sam on the bottom of his cage. She pictured Annie, rehearsing the play. Her stomach rolled.

At noon, her father sat down carefully on the edge of her bed, clutching a cup of soup. He set the cup on her bedside table.

"Okay, Charlotte," he said firmly. "This has gone on long enough. If you're this ill, you'd better see a doctor. You'll starve yourself to death."

Charlotte looked away. She didn't need a doctor, and her father knew it.

"Look," he said more gently, "I think this is about Sam. Is it?"

Charlotte blinked to hold back tears. She folded her arms.

"We're all sad, you know," Mr. Cheetham

said. "Sam was a special little bird. We loved him. But life has to go on."

"That's easy for you to say!" Against her will, tears began to flow. "You didn't kill him!"

Her father's mouth fell open. He stared as if she'd just flown in from the moon. "What does that mean?" he asked. "You didn't kill him either. You weren't even here."

"But I *wished* he was dead!" Charlotte pushed back her quilt and sat up. Now that she'd said that much, she wanted to say it all. She felt stuck to her kneecaps in gross sloggy mud and she wanted to be sucked loose. "I told him to swing himself into outer space, and that's what he did! That's not all, either. I wanted Annie to get hurt. *I* wanted the lead in the play. I was jealous of Sam and I was jealous of Annie, and I wished them both bad luck!"

Her father looked speechless. Charlotte didn't blame him. It was a terrible thing to hear from a daughter you loved. Or used to love. She started to sob. She sobbed so hard she hiccuped and gulped. The tears wouldn't stop. She felt full of sloshiness. She could cry for the rest of her life. She deserved it, too. She deserved much, much, worse.

But after a while, she did stop. She just ran out of tears. Charlotte hiccuped one last time and lay back. Her father was still staring. Charlotte closed her eyes so she wouldn't have to see him.

"Charlotte," he said finally, in a very strange voice, "why were you jealous of Annie? You were the one who wanted her to be a star. Remember?"

Charlotte nodded. She opened her eyes and tried to look at her dad. She couldn't. "I know," she said to the front of his shirt. "But it seemed like everybody forgot it was *my* play and that I was the director. Everybody just kept paying attention to Annie." It was a dumb excuse, but even now she felt a twinge of disappointment remembering how little they'd all appreciated her. "Even you," she said bitterly, finally looking into his face. "When you came to watch, you were only noticing Annie. How great she was. That's all everybody notices."

Mr. Cheetham stiffened. "I certainly was not only noticing Annie," he said indignantly. "I was watching the play. Thinking how imaginative and lively and charming it was. I was amazed I had a daughter bright enough to have written it! Every time I heard Annie say a line, I admired the line."

Charlotte sprang up so fast she bumped her head on the wall. "Why didn't you tell me?" she demanded. She'd been jealous and wicked for nothing! Somehow that made things worse.

Her father frowned. "I did! I said it was incredible, didn't I?"

He'd been talking about the play? He'd meant the *play* was incredible and not Annie?

Her father rubbed wearily at his eyes then rested his hands on his knees. "Okay, Charlotte," he said. "I guess I made too big a deal out of Annie. Without meaning to. But that's what she needed, wasn't it? I thought we'd agreed. I thought you understood."

Charlotte felt like a fool. She *had* understood. At first, anyway. Somehow she'd just forgotten.

"I really don't see how this happened," her father said. "I mean we all loved your play from the beginning. And you got to direct it and choose the cast. Right?" Charlotte nodded miserably. "So why would you feel unappreciated?"

"Because then Mrs. Sanchez took over," Charlotte remembered. "She didn't ask my opinion about a thing!" Well, that wasn't exactly true. Especially not lately. "Not much, anyway," Charlotte amended. "And she doesn't even know about my Director's Book. I did all that work and she never even read it!"

"Did you show it to her?"

Charlotte suddenly felt funny in the knees. If she hadn't been sitting down, she'd probably have fallen. "No," she admitted weakly. She didn't know why she was even complaining about Mrs. Sanchez. She wasn't mad at her now. She hadn't been, for ages.

Her father smiled, but it was a sad smile. The kind he wore when he was really disappointed and didn't want to say it. Charlotte hoped he wouldn't talk, but she could tell by the look on his face that he was going to. A lot.

"Charlotte," he said slowly, as if he were thinking hard about every word he planned to say. "A play is a joint endeavor." He didn't sound mad— just confused, that he should have to explain something so obvious. "It belongs to a group. To your whole class, including the teacher. And they're doing a wonderful job. You should be proud. You're part of the group. A very major part."

Charlotte nodded. She knew all that. She'd known it all along. How art wasn't a selfish thing. How every part in a play, even the tiniest one, was important, like Mrs. Sanchez said. Charlotte had believed it, too. Or part of her had. The other part wanted the play to be all hers and everyone to admit it. It was like she was two different people sometimes. Part of her had loved Sam and Annie and the other part had hated them both.

"You know, Charlotte," her father continued, his voice kind but firm, "I think you're old enough to outgrow this need you have to be the center of attention all the time. It's childish. And it's harmful to you—in lots of ways."

135

Charlotte nodded sadly. It was harmful to birds and best friends too. "It seems like only part of me's grown," she admitted sadly. "There's a baby part that keeps getting jealous of everyone else. I *hate* that part."

Her father ran his finger gently along her cheek. "The truth is, I guess, there's a baby part in all of us. It's probably there until the day we die. We just have to work at keeping it in check. Making it behave. We have to—"

"Baby-sit it?"

Mr. Cheetham laughed. "Exactly," he said.

"Another thing," he said when they were in the kitchen eating soup. "Wishes don't make things happen. You did not kill Sam. Ruth was careless. I wouldn't want you to say this to her, because she feels miserable enough, but she should never have left him on that tray." He shook his head. "But it's over. And it was an accident. Neither you nor Ruth really wanted any harm to come to Sam. We all know that."

"And I didn't really wish anything bad to happen to Annie," Charlotte whispered into her soup. "I didn't."

Her father passed the crackers across the table and waved them beneath her nose. "That," he said firmly, "I know."

20

Charlotte rushed upstairs to get dressed. She couldn't believe she'd been wasting time in bed when the play was only four days away! There was a rehearsal today after school. It was a dress rehearsal, too. Mrs. Sanchez must be going crazy.

At school, Charlotte stood timidly in the doorway of the auditorium and peered in. The rehearsal hadn't started. They were all running around shouting orders at each other. Near the door stood Little Witch One and Little Witch Two. Sarah was powdering them to make them white and witchy. Powder flew everywhere. It covered the front of their black dresses and their hair.

"Hey, Mrs. Sanchez!" George yelled from the stage. "I found the missing bush!" The bush was hooked on something behind the curtain. George gave a yank and it popped loose with a *boing*, unraveling as it came. Charlotte was glad her father wasn't there to see. He'd worked hours getting those bushes to look just right. Now George was rolling it back together any old way.

"Cut it out!" someone shrieked backstage. It sounded like Tina. It was Tina. She suddenly flew through the curtains in a long black bulging dress. A funny-looking fur piece dangled from her neck, and a big black hat sat on her head. Feathers stuck out of it every which way. Charlotte couldn't believe it—there stood Great Grumble Witch of the Woods. She was perfect.

Great Grumble Witch was mad. "Mrs. Sanchez!" she bellowed. "Robert and Michael keep plucking my hat! And they're eating all the trick-

or-treat candy they're supposed to carry around. They should *not* eat the props!"

But Mrs. Sanchez was nowhere to be seen. Annoyed, Tina turned and marched back behind the curtain.

"Ow!" Robert yelped.

Where *was* Mrs. Sanchez? And where was Annie?

"Charlotte? Is that you?"

Charlotte turned. The teacher was hurrying down the hallway, trailing Annie. When Annie saw Charlotte, her eyes grew round.

"Oh, Charlotte, you're here!" Mrs. Sanchez said, hugging her enthusiastically. "Thank goodness. We were just going to call your house to check on you, weren't we, Annie?"

Annie didn't answer. Her face, Charlotte saw, was splotchy and red. She'd been crying! Why? Before Charlotte could ask, the Little Witches caught sight of her and rushed into the hall.

"You're back!" Jenny said happily. She gave a little skip and thumped on her chest in relief. A cloud of powder arose.

Suddenly Tina's voice echoed from the stage. "Stop it, you jerks! This is *not* your property. I won't say it again! I told you to rehearse, now rehearse!"

Mrs. Sanchez frowned in the direction of the voice. Laura and Jenny rolled their eyes.

"She thinks she's the new director," Laura whispered. She lifted her chin in imitation of Tina. "Directing is in my blood!" she mimicked, waving an arm for effect.

Mrs. Sanchez covered her mouth to hide a smile. "I daresay it is," she whispered back. Laura and Jenny giggled.

Charlotte's ears rang. They were laughing at Tina—at the funny idea that she thought she could take Charlotte's place!

Mrs. Sanchez suddenly grew serious. "Okay," she said. "Let's get this show on the road." She waved Laura and Jenny into the auditorium.

Charlotte looked at Annie. Close up, it was clear she'd been crying. Charlotte bet anything Tina had picked on her! Or made fun of her acting!

"Did Tina do something to you?" she demanded. She'd kill Tina. She really would.

Annie shook her head and wiped at her face with the sleeve of her robe.

Charlotte didn't believe her. "I can see you're upset," she said. "You've been crying!"

Annie blushed. "Well, not because of Tina," she said. "I guess because of you. I thought you weren't coming back."

Charlotte stared. "You mean *never*? You thought I wasn't *ever* coming back?"

Annie gave an embarrassed little shrug. "Well, at least not for the play."

Charlotte thought this over. The familiar rumble started up again in her stomach. "I guess I wasn't," she admitted. "I didn't think I should. I've been a jerk, telling everybody what they should do all the time."

Behind her glasses, Annie's eyes blazed. "But that's your job," she pointed out. "That's what directors do!" Somewhere nearby, Tina screeched.

"And not like that, either," Annie said angrily. "When *you* have advice, it's for the good of the play! Rehearsals were awful when you weren't here. It was like nobody cared again."

"Hey, Charlotte!" George stuck his head through the doorway. "Mrs. Sanchez needs you in here. And did you bring the leaves? We're supposed to dump them onstage!"

Charlotte and Annie looked at each other. The leaves!

"Tomorrow," Annie whispered. "After school." Charlotte nodded.

"It's too early for the leaves," Charlotte told George, as if she planned it all along. "They have to be fresh for the show. So they'll crunch."

"Tina will be fresh for the show," George replied. Everyone laughed.

"I guess we better go in," Charlotte said to Annie. Mrs. Sanchez needed her.

21

Twenty minutes to go! Charlotte peered through the curtains. Most of the audience was already there. Her parents and Ruth and Marie were in the second row with Annie's mother. And there was Mrs. Arnold! She saw Charlotte and gave a little wave. Charlotte waved back and yanked the curtain closed. She couldn't believe it. This was really going to happen! All these kids—even Tina—were going to stand on the stage and say lines Charlotte had written. It was a miracle. Just their *doing* it was a miracle. Why had she wanted credit, too?

"Psst! Charlotte! Charlotte!" Charlotte turned around. There stood Annie in her witch's robe and her pointed hat, her face powdered a snowy white. She looked great! But something was wrong.

"I can't do it, Charlotte!" Annie gasped. "I can't, I can't, I can't!"

"Of course you can," Charlotte said quickly. "You've been doing it for weeks. You're incredible. My dad says so. Everyone says so. You'll be great." But suddenly Charlotte wasn't so sure. Rehearsing in front of the class wasn't like acting here tonight. Even Charlotte felt that. And Annie was shy. She'd always been shy. Why should she change now?

Annie shook her head and yanked off the hat. She thrust it at Charlotte. "I can't do it, and I don't want to," she said. "You do it. *You're* like Carlotta, not me."

Charlotte stared down at the hat. Hadn't she wished for this very thing to happen? She'd wanted Annie to give up the lead and let her have it. But she hadn't meant it—just like she hadn't meant for Sam to die. That had been the baby part of her talking. The real Charlotte had wanted Annie to go out and be a star. She still wanted that. If Annie didn't do it, she'd sit around her whole life long and wish she had.

"Annie," she said firmly, "we picked you for this part because you're best. Just do what my dad said. Block out the audience, okay? Start doing it now. You are Carlotta, the dot-me-magic girl. Right this minute you're Carlotta. Carlotta, Carlotta, Carlotta."

143

Annie squeezed her eyes shut and moved her lips.

"That's it!" Charlotte said encouragingly.

Annie's eyes popped open. She shook her head.

Calmly, Charlotte put her hands on Annie's shoulders. She stared into her eyes. "Carlotta, Carlotta, Carlotta," she said in a deep, steady voice. She would hypnotize Annie into being a star if she had to.

Again Annie closed her eyes. Again she moved her lips.

" 'Dot me here, dot me there,' " Charlotte whispered as Annie turned and wandered off. Her eyes were still closed, and her lips still moved. She knocked over a chair and just kept walking.

Everything else was chaos too. One of the green bushes had gotten separated from the rest, and no one could find the string to tie it with. And tubes of lipstick for the dot-me-magic scene were missing. Charlotte saw one of them roll across the floor and hurried after it. She bumped into Jenny, who was grabbing the powder puff from Laura's hand. Jenny had white splotches of powder on her hair and robe.

"Oh, my," Mrs. Sanchez said, seeing Jenny. She must have said, "Oh, my," at least fifty times in the last half hour. Suddenly she held a finger to her lips. As if by magic, everyone grew still.

144

The teacher motioned them into a circle around her. Charlotte glanced at Annie. Her eyes were open, but she looked dazed. Charlotte hoped that somewhere inside herself she was busy being Carlotta.

"Now look here!" Mrs. Sanchez drew a deep breath and gazed around. "We *must* calm down. It's almost time. I have a few things I'd like to say. First, I want you to know how proud of you I am. This has been hard work for all of us, but I hope everyone feels, as I do, that it's been well worth the effort. Something special has happened to us as a class. Have you noticed it? We've pulled together. Thanks to Charlotte, we have a wonderful play. We've also had wonderful direction. Most importantly, you've listened to her like adults."

It was true, Charlotte thought. They *had* listened, especially these last few days. It wasn't just because Mrs. Sanchez made them, either. They'd *wanted* to. The wonder of it struck her anew. She looked at them listening now to the teacher. In their costumes they all looked sort of silly—especially Tina with the feathers on her head. But Tina's costume was just right. She was trying. They were all being characters Charlotte had written, even if they had to look silly doing it, even if they didn't have the best parts. It seemed incredibly nice of them.

"Charlotte?" Mrs. Sanchez smiled at her. "I think we need one last word from our director before we go out there to knock them dead."

One last word? Charlotte swallowed hard. What word should it be? She felt as if everything would fail if she didn't say exactly the right last word.

She cleared her throat. Suddenly she knew what that word was. "Thanks," she said. "My one last word is 'thanks.' "

But it wasn't enough. They still stared. They wanted *more* last words! "Because this play is a *play*," she added. "I mean it can't be a play with just one person. It takes everybody. And everybody's helped. And listened. Even when I'm bossy sometimes."

"You haven't been bossy, Charlotte," Jenny hurried to say. "At least not too much."

Everyone laughed. Charlotte happened to look at Tina. Her face wore a funny look, like she was feeling something she didn't want to say. Charlotte suddenly knew something she hadn't known before: There was a baby part to Tina, too. Tina had been jealous. Jealous of *her*!

"So I just want to wish you luck," Charlotte added. "You're all great at your parts. Even Tina." The class laughed again, but Charlotte didn't. She meant it. Tina looked up at the ceiling and didn't reply.

"That was lovely, Charlotte," Mrs. Sanchez said. "I too wish everyone luck!"

"Luck?" Annie piped up brightly. "Who needs luck? We all have flair!"

The audience roared and clapped while the two little witches dotted themselves and recited their chant:

"Dot me here, and dot me there,
Dot me, dot me, everywhere!"

Laura got a little carried away. She took off a shoe and dotted her big toe. Tina got a little carried away too, but that was good. The audience loved it.

They booed and hissed as Morgan the Maniac planned his evil attack on innocent trick-or-treaters, and they watched nervously as Carlotta floundered around in the bushes. She gasped and groaned and beat the bush with her fist, just like she was supposed to.

" 'Drat this bush!' " she yelled. " 'How can I save the children if I don't get free? And how can I get free if I don't know my chants? Oh, woe! Woe is me!' "

They cheered when she finally pulled loose and arrived in time to stop the little witches from trying to use the useless dot-me-magic. Just in time she remembered the famous chant of Great Grumble Witch when she was a young and lively

witch. Morgan the Maniac collapsed on the spot. The audience went wild. They applauded and whistled and stamped their feet.

When it was over, all the performers came out one at a time to take a bow. The cheering for Annie was loudest of all. Annie turned bright red and hid her face, like the old Annie Block, but Charlotte knew she was thrilled. The audience liked Tina, too. When they cheered, she twirled the animal head that hung from her neck.

Mrs. Sanchez walked to the center of the stage. They even clapped for her and she took a little bow too.

"Thank you," she said. "But the one you should be applauding is our young author and director, Charlotte Cheetham. I'm sure you're all as amazed as I that a sixth-grader could have written such a wonderful, original play. Charlotte, will you come out here, please?"

Charlotte was stunned. No one had told her this was going to happen. When she walked onto the stage, everyone began to cheer again. Someone even took pictures. For a moment, she was blinded by flashbulbs and excitement; then she could see her mother and father, beaming in the second row. And Ruth and Marie. They were smiling a little too. Even Ruth, who hadn't smiled once since Sam had died.

Annie suddenly appeared at Charlotte's side.

Mrs. Sanchez put a hand on each girl's shoulder and the audience quieted down.

"Charlotte," the teacher said, "the class and I wanted to express our appreciation for this special day you've given us. It's a day none of us will ever forget. We want to make sure *you* don't forget it either, so we've had a little remembrance made up for you."

Annie took a package wrapped in white tissue from behind her back and handed it to Charlotte. A remembrance? Charlotte stared at it.

"Unwrap it, dear," Mrs. Sanchez said quietly. "Let the audience see."

Charlotte took the package and began to fumble with the paper while everyone watched. It seemed like the audience had gone home, they were so quiet now. They hadn't, though. About a hundred people were watching her unwrap this gift. She could feel every eyeball.

Annie reached for the tissue as Charlotte pulled it away from the package. Charlotte stared in amazement at what she held in her hands: a small gold plaque on a wooden background. She couldn't read the words printed on it. Everything was a blur. She had a plaque! A real gold plaque!

"If I may, Charlotte," Mrs. Sanchez said, reaching across her shoulder and holding it up. "It says, 'To Charlotte Cheetham from Her Fans in Room 8.' And there's a card from the class," she added, holding that up too. Charlotte saw names and drawing all over the back of it.

Again, the audience began to clap. Charlotte's father stood right up. Behind him, Mrs. Arnold did too. And then her mother, and Marie, and finally Ruth, as if she were attached to Marie by invisible thread. For one second Charlotte thought of poor little Sam. When she got home she was going to tell Ruth the truth—that she'd thought Sam was a great bird. A special bird. Maybe she'd even make him a plaque.

People kept on clapping and clapping. Charlotte couldn't believe it.

"Thank you," she whispered, but no one could

151

hear. Except maybe Annie. Charlotte looked at her. Annie smiled and Charlotte smiled back. She loved this plaque. She loved it with all her might. But she didn't need it. How could she ever forget this day? It was going to be her thing of beauty and joy forever, and it had settled right down into her heart. At last.

DATE DUE

OC 9 '90 2 '94			
DE 18 '90 OC 01 '99			
MY 14 91			
OC 16 '91			
OC 31 '91			
NO 7 '91			
NO 21 '91			
MR 25 '92			
OC 6 '92			
OC 22 '92			
NO 18 '92			
JA 21 '93			
JA 28 '93			
OC 20 '93			
OC 27 '93			
NO 10 '93			
OC 26 '94			

Holmes, Barbara Ware
Charlotte Shakespeare and Annie
the great